THE OTHER SIDE OF THE

THE OTHER SIDE OF THE LINE

JOE PUBLIC PUBLICATIONS

THE OTHER SIDE OF THE LINE

The time was 2002. Jip and Luci were a couple who had met whilst their circumstances meant that they were living on the road. They had a bus, which they lived on at Creach quarry. This is on the outskirts of a small Welsh village. They had both been brought up in Valleydale and they had many friends in the village. Behind the village was a giant hill.

Jip had a studio that he rented in the town; it was where he monitored the Governments antics with great interest.

Homeless people who named it The Squat occupied a house.

Being a quiet peaceful village, the population was astounded at the plight of section 48! Will they let it happen?

Jip was an acomplished songwriter and he had a heart. Being a good motorcycle rider, jip had spent years restoring his old bike.

Protesting was one caper but was Jip ready for this!

ANDY BALLARD.

THE OTHER SIDE OF THE LINE

This book is dedicated to Mrs P.E.Selley my grandmother whom I loved dearly. She was a second mother that actually put up with me as I grew up. She was always smiling and she had a warming nature.
For that solely I thank her and I wish that she could be here to read my book!

> ALTHOUGH THE DAYS ARE LONG
> WITHOUT YOUR THOUGHTS
> I COULD NEVER SURVIVE.
> ANDY.

Special thanks to Darren and Paul and all at Tower print for their help and proving that they are no 1 in printing!

THE OTHER SIDE OF THE LINE

JOE PUBLIC PUBLICATIONS
30 MACAULEY AVENUE
CARDIFF
CF3 9NW

AN IMPRINT OF JOE PUBLIC PUBLICATIONS

FIRST PUBLISHED IN GREAT BRITAIN BY JOE PUBLIC PUBLICATIONS 1998.

COPYRIGHT 1997 BY ANDY BALLARD
 Special thanks to Sioned Williams, who helped with the artwork, and to Phillip Morgan for his great photo taking skills.

ALL RIGHTS RESERVED

This book is sold subject to the conditions that it shall not, by way of trade or overwise, be resold, be hired out or overwise circulated without the publishers prior consent in any form of binding or cover other than that in which it is published and without similiar condition including this condition being imposed on the subsequent purchaser.

Printed on recycled paper and Printed in wales by Tower Print.
JOE PUBLIC PUBLICATIONS
ISBN 09 53 2988 0 9

THE OTHER SIDE OF THE LINE

THE OTHER SIDE OF THE LINE

CHAPTER ONE

It was November 7, 2002.
The light was about to peer into sight.
Alone a figure is seen sliding along a wall as if it was being hunted!
Joe witnessed this sight.
Joe was the local milkman and he was just delivering Jip's milk at his studio on Layton Avenue. This is in Valleydale.
When Joe had finished his round, he often took his breakfast in Guys café.
The Café is situated on the high street in Valleydale.
"I have had a weird morning!" Joe said.
Daisy was the waitress and Joe sprawled at her as he spoke.
"I saw a figure that was acting strange!" Joe continued.
"What did he look like?" Mr Blackett asked.
Mr Blackett was the local policeman and he also ate his breakfast at the Café.
"Well, like a woman!" Joe exclaimed.
On the next table sat Luci, she was waiting on her boyfriend Jip.
"What is it all about sir?" She gently asked.
Mr Blackett acknowledged that she was there. Then he started to say.
"It's like this Luci, a light was seen falling toward earth, but it did not land, it just hovered about twenty feet from the top of Hitchers Hill."
Mr Blackett was desperately serious as he spoke.
"What you mean U.F.O's!" Luci asked.
Jip had entered; he was there long enough to hear Mr Blackett's explanation.
"It's the governments new solar system 9000, is it not!" Jip said interrupting the police officer.
"You don't go saying that out in the open Jip!" Mr Blackett crudely said and he gave Jip a vicious stare.
Jip thought, on how he considered the policeman to be a fool.
He took a sip of the drink.

THE OTHER SIDE OF THE LINE

Luci had presented it to him as he had entered.
While all of this was going on inside, outside a busy market morning was underway; there always was a good market here in Valleydale.
Mr Marcos who was the local antique dealer, had this morning some really strange gear. Mr Dueller's the vegetable man, had all his stock gleaming clean and fresh? Nothing was any different from any normal Tuesday, except for one thing, Elaine was not at the library, and a small queue was growing.
She was soon there, she arrived in her Morris Minor car, jumping out she said,
"Sorry, I am so sorry!" She then had to run back to her car as she had forgotten her keys. She had left them in the glove box and soon retrieved them. As she ran up to the door she promptly dropped her keys onto the floor. She knelt down to pick them up when a wolf whistle filled the air. Her dress raised above her knee. The blushing Elaine finally opened the door and after a careful, half glance into the street she was at work.
Over at the local DHSS the usual routine of coffee and bacon sandwiches and the idle chat began,
"I wonder who will win today! The honour goes to the best story of today!" Tessa said to her college.
Next door was the police station and inside, they were about to serve the inmates breakfast, a couple of young hung-over men were sat in the only occupied cell,
"I saw that thing, I swear!" One of the men said,
"You were so drunk! You must have been tripping!" His mate answered.
Down the end of the road on the corner, Mrs Gill's newsagent's shop was busy with the normal papers and cigarettes hour.
Just around the corner was a squatted old building, inside everyone was asleep, so they might have been, they had spent the night taking photographs from the ridge of Hitchers hill.
Jip and Luci had tipped them off.

THE OTHER SIDE OF THE LINE

This was after a very close friend had told Jip about the solar system 9000.

At the café, Jip and Luci had finished their breakfast's and were mounting Jip's motorcycle, it was a old B.S.A Rocket 3 and it was one with a blue stripe on its petrol tank. As the engine roared into life a shout was heard.

Jip turned the engine off and gazed about, he saw his old friend Casy. "This Luci is our computer genius, Casy!" Jip said to Luci.

Casy explained that he had arrived on a Horse and cart. Jip asked him to meet him at his studio and Casy agreed.

"Yip!" Was all Jip heard as he roared away on his bike, Luci was clinging on the back as she always did.

It did not take very long before they reached the studio, once they had entered Jip turned all the electrical appliances on. This included a fax machine and a computer. Almost at once the telephone started to ring, "1 o'clock" Is all Jip heard as he answered

"It is Tuesday!" Was all that Jip said, when he had finished the call. Luci did not understand him and she told him so.

"I wasn't going to tell you because I knew you would freak out!" Jip told her.

They then slouch onto the settee and as they became comfortable a familiar knock on the door was heard.

"It's Judy!" Luci exclaimed in an excited bubbly way.

Jip observed a happy greeting.

"Good, could you both deal with the post today please?" Jip asked the pair of women.

Jip then listened to the answers on the answering machine as the women agreed.

"We have got to make sure we have the things that we need!" Was the answer he was listening too?

He went to the telephone, he dialled a number, and he stared through the glass that separated the music room from the office,

'Have you heard, they are using 9000 to plan the next route!"

He said as he made contact.
The voice on the other end of the line told him,
" I will be straight over, as soon as I am able."
Luci and Judy had began to open the letters that had arrived,
"Hell!" Luci suddenly screamed out.
"What is the matter?" Judy asked.
"It is a letter from the Ministry of Transport!" Luci said concerned.
"What does it say then?" Judy said waiting on the reply,
"At 12 o'clock Monday December 15th, the studio is to be demolished, for section 48 to fully complete its duty!" Luci stared at Jip, she was in shock!
"Yes, well I was sure it was to be soon, Valleydale is about to be part of a Government private road program, we will have to gather everyone together starting from today!" Jip told the girls.
He politely asked if Judy would telephone all of the organisations she could think of, and he asked Luci to telephone up Toby. Toby being the road protest hotline that was started after Salisbury Hill was battered in 1994.
The girls were soon at work. Jip entered his music room and he put some cushions onto the floor, he lit some incense and seven candles. He picked up his guitar and he stroked a 'Am' chord he began to sing,

> There ain't no justice in this country
> There ain't no peace at all
> They're counting everyone's virtues
> They cannot be opposed at all....

As he sang he heard the doorbell ring, he placed his guitar down.
He went to investigate. At the door was Casy.
Jip told him of the operation he was planning. While this was going on, Luci was speaking to people in Derbyshire,
"Operation Valleydale is go!" She expressed in a quiet but firm approach.

Judy was speaking with people in London and she was saying, "Valleydale needs your support!"

Meanwhile outside down at the Library, Elaine was busy photocopying for Mr Evans. She often met Mr Evans on Hitchers Hill in secret!

Then two men walked in, they had dreadlocks in their hair, Elaine stared susceptibly at them, 'Who? What?' She thought.

As she was about to speak, the door opened and Jed and Helen walked in. Elaine watched as a cuddle session began as the four greeted each other,

"Section 48" Is all Elaine hears from all of the noise.

"This may I remind you is a Library!" She stated in her firmest of voices.

The four youngsters all apologised and they headed for the History section.

"Here we are!" Helen said as she pulled out a book.

<u>Section 48 illustrated</u> the cover read.

She walked over and handed the book to Elaine,

"Helen, I can see that you are brewing today! What the devil are you up too? Protesting again?" She asked her.

"Sorry, I will tell you after the meeting" Helen replied as she placed the book into her bag and promptly left with Jed and the two dread haired men.

"Meeting?" Elaine, said under her breath, she was blown off key as Mr Evans asked,

"Tonight at the Hill, my darling?"

"Oh, err, ok" She said gently.

Back at Jip's studio, the main room was fast becoming packed full with people. Jed, Helen, and the two dread haired men were last to arrive.

When they did Jip announced,

"Great, everyone is home!" Jip reached for his glass which was full of mineral water; he took a sip,

"Let us begin, last evening at 11 o'clock, myself and Luci were here finishing up, I had the scanner on as a precaution" He said and paused.

"It was a small blip that became bigger!" Luci butted in.

"We watched it for about two hours, when it changed direction and it headed over toward the Hill! By the way any pictures yet Jed?" Jip continued.

"Not yet 5 o'clock" Jed replied.

"We have some good ones!" Helen butted in.

"Wicked! Well we tracked it and realised that this was the start of section 48!" Jip took a giant sip of the water and unrolled a projector screen.

"Switch on!" He asked Luci.

The screen flickered and an image of Wales appeared. Jip grabbed a drumstick and he approached the screen,

"As you can notice, we have the white lines here! Ha! Ha! They are in fact roads. The red hexagon is the Government appointed Record of offender store, it is where they keep tabs on everyone they consider is a threat to them, we as peaceful protesters are well amongst them, as I am sure you all are aware" Jip was rolling.

Suddenly a loud banging noise came from the door,

"I'll get it, it will be him next door!" Luci said as she made her way to the door.

Once she had opened the door she was confronted by Anthony Mullgood, a middle aged car sales representative who as everyone knew was a talk-a-holic,

"Oh it's you!" Luci said as she saw him,

"Is that scoundrel with the Horse in there! The thing has dirtied in my yard a bloody-gain!" Anthony tried his best to look angry.

Luci smiled and slammed the door closed.

"Can we get on?" Jip asked as he stared at Luci.

Luci smiled and nodded.

"Right, this orange spot here, is where the Nitro- Chlorine acid based CS gases are kept. These were confiscated from a mad bloke in the middle east in 94-95 ish, they decided the best place to dispel the gas was by taking it at a pint a time, to the top of Hitchers Hill. Because of the risks involved they are to make a bloody road! Not mind you any road, but it will be a sealed tunnel that will cut above ground around here!" Jip pointed his drumstick to Hitchers Hill, which was a easy ten miles away from the store.

"How are they to dispel the gas? If it ever gets there, do we know?" Casy asked the question.

"Yea, they plan to mix it with pure oxygen at 0:5% gas to 100% Oxygen, it would then leak out slowly up a tall tube at a pint of it a week! It is absolutely ludicrous!" Jip was shaking his head as he finished speaking.

"So what is the most prominent threat?" Jed asked.

"It's like this, first they will take all of this land from here, (Jip pointed at the map) to about here, they are not allowing anyone to be within 1 mile radius either side. This means we will lose our mountains and a lot of the Forrest. In fact it will be our freedom!" Jip held his arm aloft in a defiant gesture.

"Are we going to let this happen? For one mans madness! Are we!" Jip screamed angrily.

"It is disgraceful, but what are the alternatives?" Helen asked in a concerned manner.

"Because we and the United Nations control the Middle East, why can they not dispel it over there?" Jip spoke as he walked to the file cabinet and produced a piece of paper,

"We blah, blah, Government, blah, blah, cannot put any more lives at risk by movement of Cs one, out of the U.K."

"That's out!" Luci piped into the conversation.

"Number two, why don't they send it to space and dispel it over the centuries?" Jip talked as he again picked out another piece of paper,

"In correspondence to the idea, sub-section 2, paragraph 5.

It is and would prove too expensive, and it would involve too much time, this incurred due to the Germicidal Monocle 1996."

"That's that one!" Luci said with a frown on her face.

"Section 48 is total madness, they actually reckon, that after 200 years Wales can have it's land back, it appears to have no option but to attempt section 48!" Jip held the piece of Government file up in the air.

"This is protest like the olden days!" Casy stood up as he spoke.

"I am rather afraid that this is the big one! Mother Earth needs us!" Luci said, and then recalled of how she had met Jip at a Meat protest near Shoreham in 1994, she smiled at Jip.

Jip looked at his watch,

"We need the whole route squatted, we will need benders and vans, well everything, do we have it?" He asked.

"Yip!" Was the primeval scream.

Then as everyone was leaving Judy pointed out,

"Meeting at the Hill 2300 hours, Friday, see you all then" She gave Casy a big smile.

Once they had all left, Jip picked up his guitar and playing a 'E' chord, he started to sing,

<blockquote align="center">
So they play again
Take it all away again
We try to live in peace
We try to release....
Our land
</blockquote>

"Jip! It is ten to one!" Luci shouted.

"Drat!" Jip said as he puts the guitar down and he raced to his coat,

"Where are the keys, Luci the keys?" He stared angrily at Luci.

"Here!" Judy said as she picked the keys from the telephone table and she handed them to him.

"Thanks" Jip said as he grabbed his motorcycle helmet and ran out of the building to his bike.

"Come on baby" Jip said as he kicks the B.S.A into action.

CHAPTER TWO

Luci and Judy sat at their usual table; they could gaze out of the window onto the rear of the café. A little brook with a muddy bank surrounded the back yard. Luci was eating an egg salad roll, Judy had a cheese and onion roll, and both were sipping tea.
"How long would you expect him to be?" Luci said talking about Jip. Judy said she was unsure and the subject was closed. Elaine strolled into the café. Elaine asked the girls if she could join them and the girls agreed. Luci thought Elaine was looking concerned and she asked her,
"What is the matter with you, Lainy, was it a late night?"
"Well, what a morning I had! First my car would not start, then I caught my leggings, and if that was not enough, I bumped into Alex!" Elaine said as she stared at the brook.
"Oh well, one of those mornings!" Luci politely laughed.
As Daisy the waitress delivered Elaine's breakfast, she said,
"I saw Jed and Helen this morning did they tell you?"
"Yes, they found the book didn't they?" Luci replied with a touch of devilment in her eyes.
"Oh, it so intrigues me, what you young people get up too, section 48 indeed!" Elaine laughed and took a bite of her dinner.
Luci decided not to tell Elaine of the goings on and they all sat in silence for the next ten minutes.
Luci looked up from her cup as she heard the sound of the motorcycle roaring up.
"It's Jip, he was quick eh?" She said and looked concerningly at Judy.
"You will love this!" Jip announced as he entered the café.
"What now?" Luci carefully enquired.
"Because Ted and Beth own the studio, we have no chance of barricading it at the moment anyway.

THE OTHER SIDE OF THE LINE

THE OTHER SIDE OF THE LINE

They have just informed me that the government has put a compulsory purchase order on the property, and surprisingly, they have given them three times its worth!" Jip said.
He then told them of the meeting.
"So what does it all mean?" Luci asked, she looked at him in a despondent manner.
Jip explained that Ted had offered him a tidy sum of money to vacate the premises by Friday. Luci thought for a while and she had a small tear in her eye.
"We have to find a new studio!" Jip said as he looked at Elaine.
Jip asked Elaine if she would kindly put a postcard in her Library window, he wrote a note and put his mobile phone number on it.
"No problem young man" Elaine said smiling.
Elaine then grabbed her coat and she left the café.
Jip's mobile phone started to ring,
"Yes, 5 o'clock will be fine" Jip said as he listened.
He then finished his short conversation and he whispered to Luci,
"They have the pictures!"
The two smiled at each other and they left for the studio. When they arrived, Jip started at playing to be a sound engineer. Luci went about writing a letter. Judy decided that it was time to do some cleaning. Jip found he could not concentrate on anything, so he rolled himself a cigarette and sat back into one of his comfortable chairs,
"If only there was peace in society!" He says aloud, but nobody heard him. Jip then drifted off into his familiar arty mind.
The afternoon was soon turning into evening and 5 o'clock had came and went. The pictures had not turned up, Luci decided to ring Jed and Helen.After speaking with Jed for a while, Luci went into the music room to see Jip,
"Half an hour" She told him, he understood what she had meant and nodded his approval.The time flew by, it did not seem to be very long when there was a ring on the doorbell,

Judy was actually going home, and as she left she let a flustered Jed in. He was carrying a briefcase, he was quick to open it and reveal the picture's he had taken the night before.

"Look!" Jed said to Jip.

Jip saw about ten photographs, on them were pictures of a modern helicopter which had a very bright light beaming from the front of it's body.

"It's the Solar System alright" Jip remarked.

Jip said to Jed that the solar system was here for the job of section 48, he asked if he would be able to keep the photographs with him. Jed agreed and patted him on the back. As Jed was leaving Jip said, "Friday at the Hill."

Jed smiled a knowing smile as he closed the front door behind him.

Jip and Luci were finally alone and they stole a couple of minutes for a kiss and cuddle,

"Lets go home, I am really tired?" Luci said.

Jip and Luci both lived on a bus; it was an Albion bus. They had parked it at a friend's quarry, which was called Creach Quarry.

The days soon passed, everything was geared for Thursday and when it finally arrived, it was mayhem!

Every one of Jip's friends was busy helping remove the gear from the studio. Nobody knew where to take the possessions, so they piled them all outside in the yard.

When it was lunchtime, Jip and Luci went to the café where they met Elaine,

"I am glad that I have seen you two today!" Elaine said as she greeted them.

"I'm sorry but we are not in very good moods today, moving day!" Luci glumly said.

"Well, I have been thinking, look the Library has a basement, it's soundproof, it even has it's own entrance at the rear, mind you it has been empty for years, well since the second war!" Elaine excelled herself and she looked at Luci.

Jip thought 'The Library of all places!'

"There are five big rooms and there is a big hall, why don't you move in? Let us say £50 a week?"

Elaine spoke in her most distinguished voice.

Jip started asking her if it had it's own entrance and what kind of state it was in.

"It has a garage, as well as a private track along by the brook!" Elaine replied.

It was decided that they would all meet at the Library at 3 o'clock. They would then view the property.

All parties agreed and lunch was heartily eaten.

After lunch it was back to work for them all and soon enough the time was nearing 3:30pm. Jip and Luci left the studio and walked the 100 or so yards to the Library basement. There they met Elaine, who showed them around,

"We will take it!" Luci decided.

"Nobody in authority should know!" Elaine sheepishly said.

"In that case we will pay you £30 a week!" Jip replies wittingly.

"Oh, you young people!" Elaine laughed.

And so it was agreed.

The rest of the day was spent moving the gear from the studio, over to the Library basement.By the time Friday lunchtime had arrived and all the work was done, everything was in its new place.

Jip picked up his guitar and he sang,

The song was quite fast and he did ever so well fitting the lyrics into the complex chord structure. Love filled in his heart and his eyes slowly closed. Then his foot started to thud the up tempo beat.

Time is for the changing
Life styles are for the making
Feelings for rearranging
Emotions are up for the taking

Life is such a wonderful thing
The chatter the love
When a bird will sing
We can do anything
We can do anything.

Jip stopped playing suddenly,
"What's up?" Luci asked as she was enjoying the song.
"That book up there!" Jip said as he pointed to a book high on a built in shelf.
Luci fetched the ladder, which was hanging around. She retrieved the book, ofcourse, it was dusty, and she blew away the cobwebs. The cover read,

Intelligence Tactics 1945.

"What use is this?" Luci asked Jip.
"You will see!" Jip said as he started to read the book.
That was all Luci saw of Jip for hours that afternoon, she understood that he had a lot to work out.
The meeting was planned for later that evening! Luci decided to walk over to the café. As she trudged up the
steps, she caught Elaine's eye. She was on the telephone, and acknowledged Luci by waving her hand. Luci waved back.
"Tonight at the Hill Alex? It will be fine"
Elaine was speaking on the telephone,

'I can't wait' She thought in her broody way.

Jed and Helen were over at the local dole office, they were listening to an older man who was demanding money from the only person who was sat behind the only operational screen.

"Tonight, everyone is ready!" Jed said to Helen.

"Yes, at last we can do what we do best, LET US PROTEST!" Helen replied.

Jip and Luci had arrived home at the bus, Luci was about to light the wood burning stove when Jip walked in to her kitchen area,

"Do you want a stir fry?" She asked him.

"No! I want you!" Jip replied and he swept her into his arms and carried her to their bed.

Elaine was also just arriving home; she was running her bath. She was thinking of her first date that she had with Alex.

Later on the bus, Jip was looking at his watch,

"Its 9:30pm, we just have time to eat and then we will have to go!" He said lovingly to Luci,

"Stir fry?" Luci said and she burst out laughing.

THE OTHER SIDE OF THE LINE

CHAPTER THREE

Jip and Luci were riding into town on the motorcycle, on the way as they passed the garage; they caught sight of a couple of vans there. Jip thought that he recognised them and he drove into the garage to investigate. He was not wrong, as he approached he saw two of his friends, Tim, and John. After greeting them, he told them that they would all see each other up at the Hill.

From the garage, the journey took them passed the brook, over a bridge and up a winding lane, it was big enough for Jip's bus, but only just! As they climbed up the lane, they passed a lot of people, most were walking, and a few were pushing prams, Jip tooted his horn and saw everyone smiling. After a short while they had reached the summit. As they dismounted and the engine fell dead, all they could hear was the sound of drums and whistles filling the air. The sound was beautiful and it came from the direction of the centre of the Hill!

"Is that not home!" Luci said to Jip, holding his arm tightly.

"Magic!" Jip replied in a warm way.

The two conversed to the centre where they saw a big fire already alight, on the fire was a couple of pans full of food and Jip saw a kettle boiling away. A circle of about 50 people was all sat around the fire, each was chanting or singing, some were just humming.

"It is like the old days, like a dream, everyone back together since Twyford Down in 1994!" Jip said and his mouth watered in anticipation.

Jip and Luci went and joined the circle of people; Jed and Helen had saved a log for them to sit on. It was near to the centre, a place where most of the people could easily see them. They sat for a while soaking in the atmosphere. Both peacefully remembered when they were children. Also how they used to play up there when they were very young.

Jip then thought of the time and he glanced at his watch,

THE OTHER SIDE OF THE LINE

"15 minutes!" He said aloud.

Jip then saw John who approached him carrying a green teapot, which was steaming from each side of its lid.

"Would you care for some mushroom tea?" John asked Jip.

"Wicked!" Was his reply?

Everyone sat drinking the tea. It was Jip who started to speak first, and he pointed out to a few interested parties that the Solar System 9000 had already damaged a few trees! As they looked, they saw that the bark on the big oak tree had been worn away in places and a couple of branches were laid near to it on the ground,

"Its sad" One of the party said.

"Yes I agree, this is only the start!" Jip replied and a tear filled his left eye.

Just then someone unknown at that moment placed his hands over Jip's eyes; Jip spun around quickly and saw his friend Casy.

"Glad you could make it, have you everything?" Jip said as he greeted him.

"Yea, are you ready?" Casy questioned back.

Jip nodded and Jip laughingly stated to store order,

"11 o'clock everyone! It is time for our mouths shut and our ears open!"

The silence grew as Casy grabbed a milk crate, which incidentally he carried it whenever there was a meeting.

"Right you right on people! From this evening we are to make this, where we are sat, to the other side of the brook our new home!" Casy was good at opening meetings.

"Yip!" Everyone cried out.

"You all are aware of the Governments plan to leak potentially dangerous chemicals into the atmosphere! It is proposed to leak out here!" Casy spoke and stabbed a make shift flag into the ground.

Jip patted Casy on the back and they swapped places on the crate,

"We will fight a peaceful fight and we shall protect our insects and the animals and the birds and ofcourse our land!"

THE OTHER SIDE OF THE LINE

Jip felt in a defiant mood as he spoke.
Luci then stood next to him and she stated,
"We all have made it here!"
Most of the people raised to their feet and they all yelled,
> "Yip!"

Casy exchanged places again with Jip and he held up a piece of paper, "This is their planned route, we must cover as much as it as possible! I would appreciate if everyone could inform me of where he or she is to stage their protest. I will visit everyone in the morning with my Horse and get all of your details"
Casy loved the idea of it all.

"We have a office in the town to cover media, the police and any vigil anti groups that may think they have a chance!" Jip said forcefully.

"We shall have protection from Mother Earth as we have always had!" Luci butted in.

Again the cry of yip was heard.

Jip decided that he would speak again,

"Ok does everyone understand? If you do have any problems, do not hesitate to ask, as you are aware, peaceful protest is illegal since they made the Criminal Justice Bill an Act in October 1994, so don't expect to much compassion OK!" Jip looked frightfully serious.

"Let us have fun! Let us hold our places!" Luci shouted at the top of her voice.

The music then began drums, a mandolin, a flute, and quite a few shakers all started to play their melodic tunes.

Jip thanked Casy. He was astounded when Casy told him that even Elaine was there!

"Elaine!" Luci said overhearing Jip's conversation.
"How should I put this? When I arrived, I caught Elaine with Alex. They were having a kiss and cuddle!" Casy explained.
"Oh, com-bloody-placation's! Alex is the local councillor and he now knows what we are up too!" Jip said and he held his hands to his face in a gesture of anxiety.
Casy walked over to where Alex and Elaine were sat,
"Is this right Alex?" He asked.
"Look, I have been opposed to this retched plan from the start, it was February 1996 if I remember, I voted against it. I was obviously out voted, but I feel I might be able to be some form of help for you all!" Alex spoke in a business manner.
Jip and Luci were milling around by the giant oak tree; Jip raised his hands as a comfortable ease filled his body,
"This will be for Mother Earth, for our children, who can play as we once did!" Jip then kneeled and he kissed the ground,
"I love you Mother Earth"
He continued under his breath.
Luci put her hand on his shoulder and he stood back up. The party was in full swing, music was heard and alcoholic beverages were being passed about. Luci drank and started to gaze about. She saw Ted and Beth as they approached her.
"Good evening everyone! We have something we wish to tell you all!" Ted announced on his arrival.
"Good evening!" Jip replied smiling a childish smile.
"We are to donate £500 to the cause!" Ted said.
"That is very kind" Said Judy as she appeared with her dog she called Jade. Judy beckoned Ted and Beth to join her and they follow her to a nearby tree. They were able to see the brook and the whole of the village.
"We had no option Judy!" Ted said as they all were seated,
"There really is no need to explain anything to me!" Judy said.
Meaning that she understood why they had sold the studio.

"This is the start of the biggest protest since they stole Salisbury Hill! Be forewarned with caution!" Judy continued being rather serious.
Ted stared at his wife, neither of them spoke; they just gazed down at the village. It was not long afterwards that they decided to leave. They both smiled at the over serious Judy. Then walked over to where Jip was sat with Luci and the others. He handed Jip £500 in twenty-pound notes. After receiving the thank-you's, they headed back down the Hill.
"Well we have support nationally as well as locally," Jip said to Luci.
" I'm really tired, let us go too?" Luci exhaustedly said.
"Tomorrow we shall bring our bus up here and join the others!" Jip replied.
As they prepared to leave. Jip took a gaze around, he saw gorgeous people, each setting their new homes, and making them ready for the morning. Jip smiled at Luci as they mounted the machine,
"What a beautiful sight" Jip said, and they gazed back at the Hill.
They saw the silhouettes of figures dancing in the moonlight to the music. They also noticed the fire jugglers who were performing around a circle of night-lights; it all made for a great sight.
"Why can they not leave this alone?" Luci said with tears in her tired eyes.
"Don't you worry, they are not winning this one if I have anything to do with it!" Jip said defiantly.
Casy, John, Elaine, Alex, and Judy all watched as the rear light of Jip's motorcycle disappeared out of sight in a glimmer of red.
It was then that the happy family stated behaving as one. John was singing. He did so until he was too tired and fell asleep cuddling Judy. Elaine and Alex had decided to go there separate ways at around four in the morning,
"Thank heavens the Library is closed on weekends!"
Elaine said to Alex laughing, as she was a little half drunk.
"Shall I walk you home?" Alex asked her,
"Not tonight, I have to be thinking of our land!" Elaine said.

Alex thought that his woman was turning into an old aged hippie!
He laughed it off though and he kissed her goodnight.
"It is no secret anymore is it?" Alex said to her.
Elaine smiled and casually shook her head and walked off heading to the village. Alex walked in the opposite direction and was soon out of sight.
The next day was just coming alive at about mid-day. Jip and Luci were just entering in the bus. Jip bleeped the horn as he noticed a lot of bleary-eyed people, who were trying to get their breakfasts sorted, "I'm glad that I did not drink a lot last night!" Jip shouted above the engine noise. He then manoeuvred the bus so that the front was pointing down the Hill. It was fairly flat where he parked and after a little jacking and the placing of wooden blocks the bus was soon all level. Two other vehicles had followed Jip up onto the hill. Jip asked them to form a 'L' shape with the vehicles. This was done fairly quickly and once everything was placed where Jip was happy, it was time to unload the bus. Luci came out carrying a massive gas bottle. Once she had placed it around the back of the bus, she shouted to Jip, "Look! Tree-houses, benders, Children, The Tipi's!"

"Calm yourself! It is nothing that you have not seen before, is it?" Jip said commandingly.
"Yes, but I have never seen them on our Hill before!" Luci replied.
Luci ran up to Jip's side.
She looked at him with excitement in her eyes. As they walked onto the Hill, Jip was busy counting the numbers of people and animals,
"There are more than 300 people here!"
Jip announced being astonished.
"There are more coming!" Judy said as she joined them.
"Judy where is Casy living?" Jip enquired.
Judy asked him to guess, and Jip said that he thought he would be in or near an oak tree!
"You have got it!" Judy said and she pointed her hand across the valley to where Casy was frantically waving his arms from the middle of a 40ft Oak tree.
Jip raised his arm and he beckoned Casy to come and join him. They all stood and watched as Casy climbed down his homemade rope ladder.
He mounted his Horse, and came trotting over to them.
"Hey! What do you think of our Village?" Casy said being a little out of breath.
"It is so much better than I had expected or even contemplated!" Jip returned the compliment.
Casy started to tell Jip that they had at least 20 people living in the trees in tree houses, and that there was more being built as they spoke.
"Where is all of the wood coming from?" Jip asked amazed at the organisation of it all. Casy told him that Alex had surprisingly turned up with two lorries that was full of pallets made of wood. He also said that a farmer had donated a whole load of loose wood for burning.
"Wonderful" Was Jip's reaction.
Jip was then ready to take the task of meeting everyone. He started to walk toward where a lot of people were milling around.
Casy and Judy followed him and along the way,

Casy handed Jip a piece of paper saying,
"Here is the lay out of the village so far."
Jip started to read the paper and as he did, he saw a complete village formed. The paper contained information of everyone, ranging from their sex to their reasons for being at the Hill,
"This is amazing!" Jip said.
Jip's mind was running amok, all he could think about were things to do with sanitation, he was worried about the quality of the water,
"I need some volunteers please!" He asked loudly.
At least ten men walked over to him. Each had a smile and a ready to work image around them.
"We need toilets!" Jip said trying not to sound to bossy.
"Don't worry we can use our shovels and give manure back to Mother earth!" One of the men stated.
Jip then was told of a man they called Tabard, apparently he designed and made compost toilets that were clean and did not smell as bad as conventional toilets.
Jip thought this was a great idea and the idea was set into motion.
"We need rubbish runs and water runs" Jip told the waiting workers.
Jip was then told that the local farmer wanted all of the Horse manure and any old vegetable peelings etc.
He was also informed that Casy had organised a team of the Horse and cart men to do regular rubbish runs around the site. Also that the carts were available to carry the water. When it arrived.Then Jip saw an old friend who came running up to him.
He talked him and Luci, Judy and John into heading for the office to organise the food and the water. Jip told the workers that if they were willing. They could help around the site, then they would not mind going around helping who-ever-needed help. The men did not mind at all, they were soon seen to be busy. Jip knew he would not have to worry, as he could see that everyone was mucking in.Happiness was all around and peaceful spaces started to appear. A marquee tent that was transformed into a free café arrived later.

THE OTHER SIDE OF THE LINE

It was about the time that Jip and Luci were unlocking the door at the Library basement.
When they entered, they saw that the place was running wild! The fax  was spilling paper everywhere while the phone was ringing and the answer machine was flashing its neon light to indicate it was full!
It was madness!
The rest of the day was taken up organising the biggest protest ever!
Later in the evening Jip and Luci headed back to the Hill where they slept for the first night.
The next morning was soon to arrive, John and a few of the others were awake and had organised a fire to put a big pot of bottled water on. Once this had been achieved, they all sat staring out from the Hill.
It was such a wonderful morning, the sun had broken out, and the song of the birds could be heard. John stood up and he lent his head towards the sun. He closed his eyes, spread his arms wide and he took a deliberate deep long inhale of air,
"It is so beautiful for a winters day!"
He said.
John then saw a man emerge from the free café.
The man walked straight over to him, he asked him if he would enjoy some free breakfast! John and the others thought that it was a splendid idea, they took the man whom introduced himself as Stan, to his kind offer.

27

"This is grand!" John said as he took his first sip of Stan's famous brandy coffee.
He sat watching the village come to life.
He saw Casy climb down from his tree house and stick a bucket into his Horses face. Next to Casy was a young man who they called Doz. Next again, he saw Lisa. She was a peaceful blond woman. She saw John watching and ran over to see him. They hugged each other, they were old friends that went back a lot of years.
"It is so beautiful here, look there are more Horses!" She yelled and she pointed to the brook where a gathering of carts was.
John smiled, he gazed his eyes towards where a circle of Tipi's had been blessed and erected.
There he saw Tom, Peter, Mack and all of their wives and children. The children were running wild; John burst out with laughter,
"Look at leggy! He still cannot dress himself!" He giggled.
There was this little boy who had his jumper on with one arm in and one arm out!
His trousers were on the one leg and he kept falling over! It was a hilarious sight! Lisa saw this too, she went straight over to the child, and dresses him properly.
"Spoilsport!" John shouted laughing as he did.
Lisa did not return to where John was sat, but she walked to a nearby bender where Jesse was busy chopping wood for her fire. Jesse was a strong woman with a strong feminine spirit.John finished his coffee. When he placed his mug onto the table a voice whispered into his ear, "Site meeting dinner time."
He gathered himself together and decided that it was time to visit the site office. As he arrived, he saw that Jip and Luci had not awoken yet, he thought he would wake them. He climbed onto the bus and first lit the stove. Then placed the kettle on, then he shouted,
"A very good morning to the pair of white doves!"
There was a kind of a gargle from the rear of the bus where Jip had made the bedroom.

THE OTHER SIDE OF THE LINE

Then Jip staggered into the living area and was greeted with a steaming hot cup of coffee.

It did not take long and Luci was sat enjoying the luxury of someone else's coffee making skills. The idea was then put forward that they should all head for the Library basement. John told them that there was a meeting at lunch, but Jip already knew as he had asked for it to happen. They all walked down the Hill; taking in the fresh air and enjoying the stroll. Once they had arrived at the Library, they were greeted by two of the town folk. There was Mrs Ethel Jones; she ran the local second hand come bric-a-brac shop in the village. The other character was Mr Gallium Williams; he ran the local bakery shop.

Jip thought it to be a little odd to see these two stood at his door waiting for him to arrive!
Luci was in a friendly mood this morning and she politely asked what their business was?
"I am donating as many blankets and as much bedding as I am able to your cause" Ethel proudly announced.
"I am able to offer the pastries and cakes that are unsold each day, that is if you can send anybody down every evening?" Gallium said.
This was received with a lot of thanks and it was all arranged. Jip opened the Library basement and they said their goodbyes.
Back on the Hill, a caravan with the slogan 'SITE OFFICE' that was splattered all over the sides was being manoeuvred into a position that would be opposite Jip's bus at the now entrance to the Hill. This was to be Luci's out post. Judy was there, she had to clean the inside of the caravan as it was in a awful mess, it was full of old papers and old posters from a rally that had been held once.
Around the Hill, everyone looked to be busy. Casy had organised three Horses and carts to be at the bus at 11 o'clock. This had been Luci's plan, she had organised the deliveries of bottled water and the food. Well vegetables and nuts mainly, there was no meat! This was because the people preferred to be strict vegetarians. Around the Hill, some of the lads were busy putting up signs that read,
<u>SLOW CHILDREN</u> and others that read,<u> NO VEHICLES.</u>
Some other men were placing these signs down by the bridge and along the lane, which leads to the entrance that had now been organised.Down in the village, in the Library basement.
Jip, Luci, and John were busy printing flyers that read,
DO OR DIE...Section 48...Don't delegate...Fight for what is Right!
These flyers were to be sent to every organisation that supported the right of protest. There was many all over the country and even in Europe! Luci was busy labelling envelopes and she was loading the flyers into them. Jip's thoughts were focused on receiving the press. He thought of how this was only day two.

They were already getting big! His thoughts were that if they protected the studio as a squat then how would the press react, that was just for starters.

"Jip!" Luci called.

"Yes, what is it?" Jip replied.

"I will need at least half an hour, I want to make up a list for the meeting, its 10:30am and the deliveries are due at 11am!" She explained.

Jip asked sneakily, if he could go out and get some extra help? Luci saw that as a ploy, one of getting out of the work. She worked out that if he went to the Hill, he would not return until after the meeting, she did not want that to happen! Jip laughed and carried on with his work. Luci went about sorting out her list.

At 10:50am a loud car horn was heard outside of the Library basement door. Jip and Luci both went to investigate. As Jip opened the door, a smiling Judy confronted him. In her hands were a set of keys and behind her was a bright white LandRover jeep type vehicle, it actually looked brand new!

"Donated, kindly by Sarah H." Judy said and she handed the keys and a note to Jip.

Jip was a little bewildered, he took the keys and note. He began reading,

"Wicked it's a present from Sarah H!" Jip said after he had finished reading the note.

Miss Sarah H. was a very famous folk singer.

This gift made Jip feel a sense of security. He accepted it happily. He jumped into the driver's seat and he saw it was a Diesel engine.

He inserted the key; pressed the warmer button and the engine thudded into a rhythmic pattern,

"Beautiful!" He gasped as Luci joined him in the cab.

Judy closed the door of the basement and clambered into the back of the LandRover. Jip placed the vehicle into a forward gear and they were soon driving up to the Hill.

John had walked back earlier and was sat waiting for the deliveries to arrive. As the LandRover arrived, Jip saw that the whole place looked just like an entrance to a festival! He stopped the vehicle.
They all disembarked and they saw a busy information centre that had been formed opposite their bus. Judy climbed out of the back of the LandRover, to do that, she had to clamber over a few big boxes,
"Look at these!" She cried and she grabbed Luci's arm and she led her to the rear of the vehicle.
Inside, Luci found an array of portable office machinery. There were two laptop computers, three printers, one scanner, and a mobile fax machine! She ran and told Jip who was discussing the deliveries with John.
"Everyone's happy and really mellow," John said,
Jip smiled but all his eyes could really see was organised mayhem! Casy then approached on a Horse and cart, following him were two more.
"Good, good!" Jip repeated as he was thinking about the meeting that was to take place in about an hour's time.
Luci, Judy, and John unloaded the boxes from the back of the LandRover. Jip went over and spoke with Casy. The pair of them took a seat on the log near to Jip's bus, the first of the lorries came rolling in. It was fully laden with sacks of potatoes, carrots, onions.
Well almost every form of vegetable that you could care to mention! In hardly any time around 7 or 8 people started to unload it all onto the carts. By the time Jip had found the driver, who had wondered off to take a peep at the Hill, it was time for Jip to sign the docket. The food was loaded carefully onto the carts Jip noticed.
"Keep up the good work!" Judy is heard shouting to the working people.
Jip smiled to himself, he mentioned to Casy of how he thought Judy was a great asset to the running of the Hill.
Once the lorry had pulled out another filed into its place, before long it was 12:30pm,

"Meeting in half an hour!" Someone shouted.
The last of the lorries delivered its load of bottled water, the Soya milk and Soya produce and Casy was now busy leading his Horse down the Hill to the café,
"Come on lad!" He said as he patted the Horses neck.
"Lunch!"

CHAPTER FOUR

Picture in your mind, a Hill that was covered in trees. It had a sharp incline to the highest ridge. Below the ridge was a valley, under which were the river and the brook. If you looked from the ridge down into the valley you would of saw that there was around 200 people all gathered around the marquee tent, which was the café.
Everyone was smiling and they were all at peace.
Luci tried to gather everyone's attention, she banged some pots together fairly hard! Jip stood onto the makeshift stage that had successfully been erected, in his loudest voice he shouted,
"Good afternoon everyone, I am very pleased with the ever increasing number of people that have come to help in our pledge of freedom!"
Jip spoke of unity and of loyalty, he was quite a master at the art of peacemaker it seemed. He carried on talking of section 48, of how they were going to stop them! He mentioned the tunnel that was to surface, about 100 yards from the old studio's front door. He told of the reasons why the tunnel was to surface, one being the matter of the brook. They had to come over it rather than under it for fear of a tunnel collapse. This then brought the question up over the old studio that Ted and Beth had sold to the government,
"Do we sit back and let them demolish it! Or do we fight to save it?" He asked.
A vote was cast. The out-come was a unanimous decision to squat and protect it! It was organised so that a team of people would squat it 24hrs a day. Posters and some signs would be placed in all the windows and on the front door. This then brought the discussion into the question of publicity. A long discussion was had, the final outcome was,
"Tomorrow at 10am. Anyone, who feels that they wish to participate in the squatting action, could they meet at the studio then? I still hold a set of keys so entry will not be a problem"

THE OTHER SIDE OF THE LINE

Jip spoke with a sense of pride.

Luci then started the cheering and Jip stepped off of the stage. Luci passed him as she stepped onto it. Clearing her throat she said,

"The first thing I would like to mention is the, circumference of the land that we are holding, I will call this occupied land, we will have to create boundaries and on each one we will have to place a outpost tent. So whoever is interested in the job of border control on the outer levels. Please could they make themselves known at the site office?"

Jip was really impressed at Luci's speech, he did not want to stop her as she continued,

"Next, we will need information tents that will be manned all the time! We will need these at every entrance" She said.

Luci continued talking about the set up and she told everyone that she was to be chief secretary, she asked for understudies and some caretakers.

"I have noticed that Casy does the morning and evening rubbish runs with his cart. I would like to see some help for him, thank you! The last point that I want to raise is the Talking circle club; Judy has come up with the idea of meetings where people can discuss anything with others, three evenings a week? The agenda will be put up in the site office if you are interested" She informed everyone.

Judy decided that it was her turn to speak and after hinting to Luci, she took to the stage,

"As some of you are aware, we have organised the printing of petition sheets, so anyone, who wants one, could they pick them up at the site office?" she held aloft a copy of Jip's handiwork.

Jip then stepped onto the stage and said,

"Last but far from least, is there anybody who has any knowledge of the local MP's, could they make themselves known to either myself or Luci, thank you!"

Jip then burst into laughter as he saw a group of people who had dressed as clowns.

A couple were on stilts and they were miming some very funny antics as the MP's were mentioned. Then music started to fill the air.

"I do think that we have bored them enough!" Luci said to Jip as he stepped off the stage.
Jip lit himself a cigarette and he put his arm around Luci. As he did Alex appeared, he said,
"Ah! Found you finally, is there anywhere quiet where we could talk?"
Jip said they could go to his bus and Alex accepted. Jip, Luci, Alex, Judy, and John all started the walk to the entrance area. Along the way Alex told Jip that he had to meet a couple of friends that he had brought with him at the bus. Jip was wondering if Alex had brought trouble, as he was a councillor.
"Quite the contrary my dear fellow" Alex answered.
Jip thought of Alex as weird. Behind the two men was Luci and as they were walking, she was busy asking everyone that she saw, if they wanted to sign the petition or pick one up, then they should follow her! Jip soon noticed that a crowd was following them,
"I am over in the site office if you need me!" Luci shouted as she walked over to the caravan.
As she did, Alex darted over to a car which was parked in front of Jip's bus.
"I will meet you in the bus" Alex said to Jip.
"Fine just fine!" Jip said as he entered the bus.
Alex knocked on the window of the B.M.W car and the doors flew open straight away. There appeared four persons; one being female and they all wore suits. Jip entered the bus and placed the kettle onto the stove. He had a quick go at tidying his hair so he could look smart! Alex then knocked the door of the bus,
"Jip are you there?" He shouted.
Jip invited them all to go aboard, they all entered. Jip felt he wanted to run away, as he felt a little uneasy. Alex soon put him at a better ease as he introduced each person separately.
The first to be introduced to Jip was a solicitor by the name of Michael; Alex assured Jip that he was soon to be a barrister.

The next person was introduced as Jack who was the towns court clerk. The third person was Emily, Jip had a bit of a shock when Alex introduced her as the mayoress! Jip quickly made a simple bow only to be told,
"Don't be silly! We are here unofficially" She said and gave Jip a knowing wink of her eye.
Jip felt more or less at ease after he had heard Emily and her statement. Alex then introduced him to a man called Joe,
"Hi! I am a professional photographer, freelance actually!" Joe told Jip.
"Well you are expected" Jip replied.
Joe then told Jip that he would not take any photographs until he was given the all clear from him. Just then Luci arrived at the bus, she asked if everyone would care for a drink of coffee. She was a bit put off though as they all accepted, she thought that she might not have enough cups!
"Right shall we get down to our business?" Emily said and she produced a document from her bag that she was carrying. The document was a official photocopy of the letter that the local council had sent to the Lord who had put his signature to the draft of approval for section 48 to take place. It was a total refusal of any kind of help from the Valleydale council! Jip glanced up and as he took his eye from the paper, Michael the solicitor said,
"I have lived locally for around 40 years, I feel that inside of my mind that I will never support any destruction of any of our beauty spots."
The meeting turned into a special one, each of these important people pledged their support, Emily said in a calm manner,
"There is a one way vote in the council, everybody is in favour of supporting a refusal of policy! This will be the first time ever that this council has acted to refuse to co-operate with the county council and it's sacrifices!"
The meeting continued well into the evening. It had been dark for at least four hours when the party finally left the bus.

It was a friendly parting and Joe had the last words when he said,
"See you tomorrow Jip!"
When they all had gone, Luci turned to Jip and she said,
"They are not going to have this Hill, are they?"
"We are going to win! We have support nationally as well as locally as I have told you before!" Jip said being touchy as he was now very tired.
They were both soon tucked up warm in their bed sleeping.

CHAPTER FIVE

The next morning was a typical Welsh winter's day, it rained non-stop, and it was blowing a forceful gale. The rain had awoken Jip and Luci earlier and they had made there way to the café that was in the village.
"It's brilliant! Everywhere that I look! I see posters telling of the plight of the Hill!" Luci was feeling positive this day!
"It is just what we need! Support!" Jip replied. He was feeling proud inside as he saw his artwork on the walls.
Elaine then entered the café, she was smiling, and she gave them both a cheery wave. As she approached the usual table she shouted quite loud,
"How are the hero's this very morning!" Then she laughed.
Luci looked at Elaine and all she could think of was pictures of Alex and her!
"I have made a decision!" Elaine firmly said as she sat at the table.
Jip looked up and stared at Elaine as she continued,
"Myself, and the library are joining you! Go and have a look at the big front window! You can have the use of our photocopier for free!"
She sounded as if she was over excited!
They all laughed and shook hands, it was nice for them to wake and feel as if they had achieved something. Jip and Luci thanked Elaine and before they left, Jip offered to give Elaine a lift! Luci was not impressed as it meant that she would have to travel in the back of the LandRover. She considered it as bumpy! Conversation on the short journey was about the LandRover and how nice it was! Luci sat passively in the back, waiting.
When they did arrive at the Library, Jip could not believe his eyes! Elaine had positioned posters and copies of the petition everywhere! She had also written in large letters spreading across the big front window.

SAVE OUR HILL!

THE OTHER SIDE OF THE LINE

"Is that Christmas snow?" Jip politely asked.
"That was all I could find!" Elaine said bubbling along.
"Brilliant! Wow! It is a work of art!"
Luci said being slightly sarcastic, yet she really was impressed!

Jip hugged Elaine in a friendly gesture and he pecked her on the cheek. Elaine blushed.
"Yes, well, off to work!" Elaine said as she made her way into the Library.
Just as she approached the main door the postman arrived in his van, he was shouting out over to the Library,
"I have bags of post for you!"
When he had opened his van, he produced two post-bags that were crammed with envelopes.
"They are all for Jip and Luci I am afraid Elaine!" The postal worker said as he handed the bags to Jip.
"Thank god!" Elaine said as she entered the Library.
Luci was excited and she helped Jip to load the bags onto the back of the LandRover, they had to hurry as the rain had started again! Jip drove back to the bus and when he arrived, the post was taken to the site office. Jip left Luci in the office with Judy.
"We have our work cut out today girl!" Luci said to Judy as they organised their workspace.
Jip started to walk towards his bus, he saw Casy was standing close to his bus having a conversation with John. Jip's attentions then spilled onto a motorcycle, which was being rode toward him.
"Jip! It is I, Joe!" The stocky rider blurted out over his helmet chin guard.
"The bag gave you away!" Jip replied.
Joe then dismounted and stood next to Jip; he seemed to be awaiting orders! Jip led him onto the bus, sat down on his settee, and gestured Joe to join him,
"Have you seen the village yet? It is quite a sight I promise you" Jip said.
"The first job then?" Joe asked.
"Tell you what, if you start taking the pictures at the library. Then, I will see you at the basement. In about an hour?" Jip had his day organised.

Joe agreed and he headed off on his motorcycle, strapped to him was his black holdall, which carried his photography gear.

"Nice bike!" Jip muttered as he watched him leave.

Jip then went over to the office to check if there were any messages, there was a couple, he took them in a note with him. He jumped into the LandRover and drove to the Studio, he looked at his watch and saw it was 10am. As he arrived 30 or more people greeted him. They were all waiting outside the front door.

"Here we go!" Jip said as he walked over and inserted the key into the lock.

The door unlocked and they all walked in. The first job for everyone was to secure all of the windows and all of the doors. John was there and he had organised a giant banner, which he was arranging to hang up. Things became rather busy, by the time the banner was being stretched from one window to the next, Joe had arrived, and was soon clinking away at his camera,

"It's great, just great!"

He kept repeating, as he took picture after picture of the squat.

Jip asked Joe, how did he find him. Joe told him that the woman at the Library told him where to go. Jip knew whom he meant.

Jip then saw that everything was in order and everyone was helping to organise the new squat.

He decided that it was time to go to the Basement, he quietly slipped out of the rear door, and he leapt into the LandRover. He was thinking of how he was missing Luci.

Once he had reached the basement he headed straight for his guitar, he sat down and he began to play and sing,

> Today is so easy to rule upon judgement
> Easy to rule upon thought
> Let nothing place you on your back foot
> Learn for what you are taught

A knock on the door disturbed him, when he answered it, he saw it was Joe!

"I am so excited, it's a fantastic set up! It is a shame it's raining though!" Joe said as he entered.

"It is winter!" Jip said trying to be nice.

"What is your thought about the studio?" Joe asked.

"Well, we have got ten days before the diggers are due to arrive, that means that they should have the tunnel at surface level by Tuesday next!" Jip replied.

"I am impressed! It seems that you have the support of everyone around here!" Joe was overwhelmed and he let Jip know.

The two men then discussed Joe's meeting with Elaine. Jip asked him about his involvement with the mayoress. Joe explained that he was going to marry her, once she had finally left her husband. Jip did not want to hear much more as he asked Joe to follow him.

As he left the basement. They returned to the squat and along the way, they saw the milk float, which the other Joe had decorated with posters, and a banner that read, S.O.H.

Jip giggled as Joe started taking pictures of the float. Soon they arrived at the squatted studio. On entering, Jip asked John if Ted had arrived. He wasn't to sure of how well Ted would accept this action and he knew that he would turn up today for sure!Jip looked about, he saw makeshift tents for people to have their personal space, there was an information corner being set up. He was happy in the way it was coming together.

"The telephone is still on until Tuesday" Jip said as he walked passed the phone.

Everyone knew that Tuesday was also going to be the day that they would expect some kind of confrontation. Jip decided to have a glance at his old music room. To his astonishment when he entered, he was surrounded by some of his oldest musician friends! They had come from all over to see him.

First they had visited Luci, who in turn told them of Jip's whereabouts.
"Luci has sent your guitar down!" He was told as he is handed his guitar.
Jip pulled the door closed. As he gazed about the room, he could see a lot of old instruments, there was Rex who had a set of conga's and an African drum, and Jerry was there with a digeredoo, John had his silver flute and Suzie was about to play the Violin. Peter was setting up to play his Mandolin.
Jip found a spot to sit and once he had achieved that, he started to play a C chord, a G chord followed by a D chord. Most musicians would explain that this pattern is easy, but it is a good start for warming up!The music flowed for a while, until Jip decided that he would begin to sing.

> I can feel the rain
> It fills my heart with pain
> Yet from inner feelings to the world
> I see a bright horizon, a free world
>
> So I'm going to save the planet
> I'll do something-green everyday
> I won't eat any produce
> I won't believe what they say
>
> If everyone takes it a step at a time
> You will respect till the end of the line
> Mother earth will hold straight that's true
> Cause the law of nature runs the likes of you
>
> So ya gonna save the planet
> Do something green today
> Not eating no perfume don't listen to what they don't have to say

Jip continued to play for a few hours, actually it was until someone shouting disturbed him, Jip placed his guitar down and smiling he left everyone, they continued to play music. Jip went to where they had made a kitchen area; there he met Ted, who was smiling proudly,
"What a great idea of yours Jip!" Ted said.
Jip asked him if he would want the money he had gave them back? Ted told him not to be silly and that he was happy with the deal all around. Ted gave Jip another set of keys for the studio, he shared a few dates, and time's that he had heard to him.
Back in the site office Luci and Judy were busy opening the mail. The girls were enjoying themselves, as many the letters were kind donations from other left wing organisations,
"It's Christmas already!"
Judy shouted as she picked another envelope to open.
Over in the Library basement the telephone rang, no one was there so it was ringing to itself. Elaine could not hear the telephone that was below her as she was busy gathering all of the signed petitions
that she had collected. She had decided to deliver the signed one's to Luci at the hill. She had quite a bundle as she left. She jumped into her Morris motor car and she drove to the bus.
Once she had reached the site office, Elaine handed the petitions over. Luci and Elaine started a discussion about the delivery and handing over of the petition. To whom?
For Luci it seemed as if everyone had known before her that it was to be herself and Jip, who were to deliver the final numbers to, 10 Downing street...London.
This would mean that Luci would have more work to do! She had to organise the whole issue, it was too late into the day to start, so she decided and took her work back to the bus with her.
Jip, Joe, John, and Casy all decided that it was about time they all went out for a beer. They all leapt into the LandRover, and as they were leaving, so was Elaine! She nearly had a collision as she reversed her car. That diverted and she was on her way!

Jip laughed as he manoeuvred the LandRover, he drove down into the village following Elaine for a bit, he drove to the local pub, which was called 'The Valleydale Arms'

As the four men entered the public house, they were greeted by all of the people who were cheering them! Some people were clapping and the proprietor shouted over all of the noise,

"First ones are on the house boys!" He passed Jip a strong lager.

Jip had once drank in his pub everyday! John had the same. Joe had a small bitter Shandy and Casy had his usual, which was a pint of Guinness. Jip rolled himself a cigarette, he then took a sip of his pint, and he felt relieved. Jip thought of how the local police officer, Mr Blackett would often pop his head in on his way home from work.

Conversation flowed after about the third pint, the original table they all sat at had been added too, it was now four tables long.

There was around twenty people sat around. The spirit was on a high note as each were laughing and having fun!

Back aboard Jip's bus, Luci was sleeping, as she had to have a busy next morning. Elaine was home and she was preparing to meet Alex.

At the Hill, everything was a normal a night could be. The café had a Tribal dance band that was playing that evening.

At closing time, Jip was drunk, he had not seen the police officer when he had entered and left straight away discreetly.

"You're not driving are you Jip?" John asked being drunk as well.

"No, Joe is!" Jip said hoping that Joe was sober!

Joe was! He had only had two pints in four measures of Shandy! He drove the LandRover back up onto the Hill.

Once they had arrived. Jip wondered off to the café, John and Casy followed him while Joe checked his motorcycle.

They all could hear the music, which was blaring out, and they saw a large number of people had gathered.Jip walked around the tent to the rear and he fell headfirst as he tripped on the lip, which surrounds the door of the marquee tent!

THE OTHER SIDE OF THE LINE

As he raised himself from the floor he saw two burly men, they grabbed him to steady him, they led him over to a table. Jip saw a makeshift bar, he thought that he had never seen it before! Jip then saw a blond woman who emerged from out of a posh van, which was parked at the rear of the tent. Jip saw a bottle of champagne. He then recognised who the woman was!

THE OTHER SIDE OF THE LINE

CHAPTER SIX

Jip sat at the table, his head was spinning, all around him was quiet for a second, well until the band started to play another song. The band was rocking! Jip thought as he saw John who was lurking around.

"Fancy playing?" Jip was asked.

Jip replied that he would need about a half of an hour to sober up, he then changed his mind and asked for a beer! He was handed a can of his favourite brand lager. On drinking the can, he felt better and he started to roll himself a cigarette.

"Try some of this," Somebody said as they gave a piece of dope to Jip.

They became nicely stoned and as he was feeling more relaxed Jip said,

"Let's play!"

After Jip had finished his request there seemed to be mayhem all around him, there appeared about five men who were carrying musical instruments.

"You're going to love this!" Jip is told as someone places a cigarette paper that was folded in a small square, they put it into his mouth and Jip swallowed it with a sip of beer!

"Jip are you ready?" John asked as he joined him. John was holding his trusty old flute and he was beaming with excitement. He patted Jip on his shoulder and he said, "Come on, let us go and show them what were worth!" Excitedly, Jip entered the stage area, along side of him was the blond woman, she was wearing a dark hood to hide her face. Palti the clown had filled in when the other band had finished, he saw that the next band was ready and he finished this part of his act.

Jip and the others stepped onto the stage, they picked up their instruments, Jip walked to the microphone.

He stared at the crowd, then at the bass and drum players. He nodded and said.
"Ladies and gentleman! Give us a cheer for Sarah H!"
Everyone started to play, The crowd went wild, as Sarah H. was a famous singer. She was currently at number five in the pop charts! The place felt as if it was alive!
Everyone was enjoying the music.
After the band had played four of Sarah H's songs, Palti the clown ushered them off the stage and he was saying,
"They will be back after a short break, I do hope that it is not a leg though!"
The crowd roared with laughter and even more so when Palti said,
"We don't want them back legless, do we?"
Back in the rear of the stage, Jip had met Luci who had heard the music and came to hear her beloved Jip, the two were hugging when Sarah H came and sat at the table where they had seated themselves. Jip introduced Luci to Sarah and was given a towel to wipe the moisture from his face.
"This is great, just great!" Sarah said in a happy manner.
It was about then when Joe walked in and he had his camera with him,
"Can I take some pictures please?"
Jip gave him a nod of approval and the crowd could be heard shouting,
"Bring on the band!"
This chant began when Palti went into his standing on his head trying to drink a pint of beer!
In the crowd was, Ted and Beth, Elaine was with Alex and Casy had met a young girl, everyone was full of joy,
"It's just how it used too be back in the old days!" Ted said to Elaine.
"Knock, knock?" Palti said trying to save his act through the chanting!
John walked into where Jip was sat.

On his arm he had a very pretty young woman,
"This is Nancy, she plays the whistle" John said as he introduced her.
Jip and Luci giggled and went back to a cuddle.
"Time to see if the band has got plastered yet!"
Palti said as he finished his act.
Jip, Luci, Sarah, John and Nancy all squeezed onto the make shift stage, Jip grabbed the microphone he told everyone about the reasons why that they were there on the Hill and he introduced a beautiful Folk song of Sarah H's which was called,
Can't stand society all about.
The song was beautiful and Jip was enjoying it so much, he played his guitar better than he had ever played it before! John played his heart out on his silver flute and there was a fiddle with electric pick-ups that was playing, it was Luci! Sarah felt this and she sang magically, Jip found it exceptionally easy to harmonise with her.
Behind the stage was a team of engineers who were busy checking that all the instruments were playing properly.
By the time the band had sung two songs, it was as if the whole population of the Hill had turned up to watch! There were many children who were dancing; it was such a great event!
The band played on all of the night. It was around seven o'clock that morning. They finally finished. They were all, as you would expect, very tired. Casy had turned up with his Horse and a flat bed cart. Jip, Luci, Sarah, John and Nancy and four burly minder type fellows all climbed onto the cart. Casy decided that the one Horse would not be enough to pull them all, he quickly ran and he fetched another. Once he had harnessed the two Horse's to the cart, they peacefully trundled up the site heading towards the office and Jip's bus.
Jip was staring up the Hill to his bus and he saw a car, which was parked close to it.
 As they became closer, Jip saw that the car was a police car!
"Just what I need" He said under his breath so that no one could hear him.

Luci saw the police car and being a little organised, she rang the site office with the mobile telephone she always carried. She spoke with Judy who told her that there was no need to worry and that she would explain to her the facts later in the day.

Luci turned the telephone off and she settled into Jip's arms cosy like.Casy walked the Horses, they seemed to be enjoying themselves as they pulled the cart.

Casy remarked on how dry the ground was,

"We had a slight frost earlier," He said looking up at the sky.

Nobody spoke until they reached Jip's bus. When Jip rolled off the cart, Mr Blackett the police officer confronted him,

"Jip, you play ball with me and I will play back! I do not want anyone going into the village today and causing a fuss as its market day today!"The policeman said and he turned and jumped into his car and he drove away.

"If he can go to the village, then why can't we!" Jip said as he staggered on to his bus.

Judy saw them all arrive, she followed Luci onto the bus, and she placed the kettle onto the stove,

"It's market day Judy!" Luci stammered to Judy.

Judy said that it would be a good day for distributing the petition and some posters around the folk who would visit the market.

Luci smiled at her and she made a beeline for her bed. Jip joined her and the rest found space to sleep in the bus. Judy went about organising the village run, and she spent the day going to and from the busy market, making sure the police officer did not see her!

The days soon passed peacefully and it was not until Jip had news from Alex of the contractors. It was Tuesday, Jip had organised the road that entered the town to be blocked. He had organised the men to move big rocks into the road and he had parked his LandRover at the front! On top of his LandRover Jip had placed two giant speakers that he had installed onto the roof to act as a personal announcement to the LandRover.

Behind him, were some other vehicles from the Hill. Jip and Luci were sat in the front seats nervously waiting. Jip had put on some light music, which he played through the P.A. It was quite lucky that he had left some music tapes in the LandRover.

They all sat for hours, it was not until the early hours of the next morning when in the far distance, a yellow flashing light was seen.

"Here we go! Please remember we are peaceful protesters and we are Non-violent!" Jip said through the P.A.

There was sudden silence as everyone had no idea of what they should expect, Jip turned on the LandRover headlamps, and the other vehicles followed suit.

THE OTHER SIDE OF THE LINE

CHAPTER SEVEN

Could you imagine, you were driving along the Welsh countryside, it is the dead of night. You turn a corner and are confronted by glaring vehicle lights that are in the middle of the road, as you became closer, you would have saw people holding banners and you would not have anyway of passing them.
That was what Gregory the digger truck driver saw! He quickly stopped his truck and dialled his boss on the truck's telephone. His boss told him to turn around and go back to the base,
"This could turn ugly" Were the exact words of his boss!
Everyone watched in total amazement, the truck did a very peculiar turn around and then drove away.
Opened mouthed, Jip ran to the Hill, he told Luci that he was going to fetch his motorcycle and that he would follow the truck. Luci understood him and she sat peacefully in the LandRover. Suzie who was in the vehicle behind Jip's saw Jip run off and she took his place in the LandRover,
"What do we do now?" She asked Luci.
Luci told her that all they really could do was wait. They saw Jip'srear light of his motorcycle as it zoomed over the hilly landscape.
It was about an hour later when the first police-van arrived. It just pulled onto a verge opposite and sat there. Inside there was about a dozen police officers!
"Please don't do anything that will offend them, we are people just the same!" Luci said over the P.A.
Jip was returning back after he had found where Gregory had drove his truck. Jip had suspected that the contractors were close by and the site was only about ten miles from the Hill.
Jip rode back to the Hill, he used the back way as he saw a light on the Hill, which he understood to be a signal telling him to go the back way There was now around four or five police vans and they were all parked on each side of the road, opposite the protesters.

THE OTHER SIDE OF THE LINE

Jip joined Luci and Judy. The atmosphere was tight as neither side really quite new what to do! There was no communication from either of the parties. Jip turned to Luci and he said,
"It is know 8:30am, I bet you they wont contact us?"
Luci stated that she thought they would and it was to be about 9am when they would. Jip laughed at her suggestion, as he knew he would have to contact them first. In the rear of the LandRover Casy was busy making some of his famous Leek soup, he was using a gas
burner to warm his brew. People were mingling; some were eating while others were sipping hot drinks. Jip gazed about and had an idea! He reached for the mobile telephone and he found a number on a scrap of paper that was in the LandRover. He dialled the long number and once the call was connected he heard,
"Sorry, there is no one in the office to accept this call, if you need, leave a message after the tone."
"If you want news! Valleydale is happening!" Jip shouted down the phone.
Jip listened as a voice answered,
"Hello! What is this Valleydale?"
Jip explained briefly of the action and he described the sight. The voice promised a camera crew straight away, he said that they were already on their way as they spoke. Jip turned the telephone off and he muttered,
"That's show-business!" He smiled as he said this.
Jip and Luci had not noticed, behind them the whole of the village had started to arrive, the schoolteacher had brought her pupils and there was even an Age concern van full of pensioners who had joined the protest.
Jip thought for a while and he decided that it was time to contact the police officers that were sat intimidatingly opposite them.
He asked Luci if she would turn on the P.A. Luci did and she placed the microphone into Jip's hand,
"Good morning everyone, especially the one's in the funny colours!"

He said as he saw a bunch of people that were dressed as clowns, they were juggling in front of the LandRover.
"We are here to save our Hill!" Jip shouted.
"Yip!" Was the large shout from the people that were behind him.
Jip prepared to speak again, as a police officer emerged; he was wearing a peaked cap and carrying a large megaphone.
"We are the police. What you are doing here is illegal. If you all go back to your homes peacefully, we will forget that this incident had happened!" The policeman tried to sound friendly as he yelled through the megaphone.
Jip considered the statement to be foolish, but he kept the comment to himself! Jip stepped from the LandRover with the microphone, which was on a long lead,
"We have in our possession, petitions from the people who support our actions! We wish to speak with the secretary of State!" Jip was trying to be forceful as he spoke.
Some of the protester type people decided to play music on their instruments and some started to sing as the conversation was slashed. The police officer had nodded his head and returned to his van.
Casy and John joined Jip,
"They won't do anything until they have received their orders!" John said as he saw Jip.
Then as John finished his sentence, two police helicopters appeared over head and another which had Blat T.V. written on the side of it joined them.
"Don't be intimidated!" Jip said over the P.A.
Nobody seemed to be as most of them were still having fun!
The next few hours passed by calmly and Jip fell asleep for about an hour. Well until he was awoken by a knock on the window that he was sitting nearest. It was Alex and Joe!
Alex explained to Jip that the police wanted a spokesperson to go and see them and speak with them in private.

THE OTHER SIDE OF THE LINE

Jip thought about it and he agreed saying,
"After we have our lunch!"
Alex laughed and he joined Jip and the others eating a bowl of Leek soup! They discussed matters, it was decided that John was to handle talking with the press, he did not seem to mind, and he suggested that as many people who wanted to air their views would be allowed too! Jip and Luci were to speak with the police and afterwards they were to organise a field group to watch over the police activities,
"Just in case they play dirty!" Casy quoted.
After lunch and a smoke Jip and Luci were ready to speak with the police. Alex walked over to a bell tent that the police had erected on the verge. He was gone about five minutes, Jip and Luci stared at the tent from the front of the LandRover waiting. Then with everyone watching, they emerged and went over. Luci held Jip's hand tightly and he softly told her not to worry. Soon they were at the entrance to the big white tent; Jip looked back and saw that everyone had their attention on them. He swung the canvas door open and they both entered. Inside they saw a table with three highly ranked police officers sat at it. Another man in a grey suit was there too.
"Good afternoon?" Jip said smiling, he was trying to be polite.
"What do you plan to do next?" The tallest officer questioned him.
"We are planning to stay for as long as it takes for section 48 to be disbanded" Jip tried to be proud.
The police officer then introduced the man in the grey suit as Mr Evans the contractor.
"Is that it stale mate?" Jip said,
He was becoming angry at the ridicule of it all.
"We are awaiting a reply from the Secretary of State, how many women and children are you strong?" The police officer asked Jip with a weird look in his eye.
"Look it is no use us pretending! We are over a thousand people strong! All we want is justice! Peaceful Justice!" Jip was in no mood to mince his words.

THE OTHER SIDE OF THE LINE

The police officer wrote on paper and finally said,
"Fine, we will contact you a bit later."
Jip gave the police officer his mobile telephone number, and he promptly walked out holding Luci by her hand.
As they emerged from the tent, they heard cheers of ' Nice one', and other supporting shouts. Jip and Luci started to walk back to the LandRover and as they were, a car was heard revving its engine
behind them, Jip swung around and he was approached by a woman holding a microphone and a man pointing a camera at him.
The woman asked,
"We understand that you are protesting against section 48, as we have heard, the Government has arranged this without consulting the people of the village?"
Jip thought of how familiar the woman was, and he came to the conclusion that he had seen her on the Telly before! His words rolled off his tongue and he soon had the television crew taking pictures of the clowns and jugglers. He thought that it must have looked like a carnival parade!
John was in the thick of the action; he talked to the woman and was showing her about. Jip calmly stepped aside and joined Luci who was sitting in the LandRover. She asked him if he had a telephone call yet, this was her way of showing her nervousness Jip thought.
"Hey! There is a game of football on!" Casy shouted as he ran with one of the youngsters kicking a football.
Soon all of the children who liked football were playing, Jip ran to kick the ball. As he did he kicked the ball against the LandRover and it rebounded over towards the police line.
Young Albert ran to retrieve the ball, one of the police officers saw this and he picked up the ball and passed it to him. Albert politely thanked him and the police officer smiled.
The hours passed and it was around 6:30pm when most of the village folks decided it was time for them to leave. It was just becoming dark and a few were worried for their safety.

It was then that the mobile phone rang inside the LandRover. Jip was dozing and the noise awoke him.
"I am afraid that you will have to move! You are blocking a highway and this is contrary to section 5b of the public order bill!" The voice said as Jip turned the phone on.
"Don't you understand? We are not allowing any section to even start!" Jip said not liking the attitude that he heard.
There was an eerily silence for a moment, then the voice spoke again, "Ok, Then we will have to sort out some form of deal! This is because of the public's concern over this matter."
"What kind of deal are you thinking of?" Jip replied being very suspicious of the statement.
"The tunnel is due to raise to surface level in the morning, if it does and there isn't the man power or the machinery there, it will cause a life threatening position. I think you will understand when I tell you that if the tunnel is not cut in properly and we have rain, the whole of the village will be in danger of collapsing into the hole!" The voice sounded ever so serious.
"You will have to give us some time?" Jip asked needing time to discuss the reason with the others.
"This is not a laughing matter and all we want is a peaceful ending the same as you! All it will take is a little co-operation from you all!" The voice finished and the phone went dead.
Jip could not believe what he had been told, but he felt he had to play along with the plan.
"Bloody typical, I did not think that they would have to seal the tunnel. The walls would collapse and water would deteriorate the sides and this would cause it to collapse! This would because of the closeness of the village, cause a landslide! What is next?" Jip sounded defeated as he spoke to all who were listening.
Luci went and she gathered all of the people who were still at the protest together.

She directed them to the LandRover where Jip was waiting. Jip told them the entire dilemma, it was put to the vote, and it was voted that the action was to be cancelled!

"We really have no choice but to let the workers in!" Jip said as the tears began to appear in his eyes.

Casy noticed this, he went over and put his arm on Jip's shoulder, and he said,

"We will have to go to plan B! We will hold the squat!"

John was listening and he looked straight at Jip when he said,

"They don't need to demolish the squat, so that they can seal the tunnel do they?"

Jip agreed with John, Jip was a little happier as he realised that even if he had to agree for the contractors to come in, he did not have to hand over the squatted studio!

Another hour passed as the discussion grew; the mobile phone then started to ring again.

"Have you made a decision?" The voice asked.

"We have, as we are peaceful protesters we don't want any harm to come to any others. We will let you seal your tunnel; we are not though going to allow you to demolish the studio! This will be squatted and we shall not move from the Hill until section 48 is dropped!" Jip was annoyed and it probably sounded it to the policeman.

"The road must be clear by mid-night tonight! I need your word that this will happen!" The voice was less provoking this time.

Jip told him that he promised this would be possible.

The telephone then was still again. Luci switched the P.A. on and Jip told everyone of the plan. Most already knew, and they started to move all of the rocks and the vehicles started to clear the road. Everyone then either went to the squatted studio or they went back to the Hill. Within half an hour the road was clear and from the squat, lights were seen as the police formed a barrier around a sealed space opposite the squat.

Jip and Luci went to see Elaine and Alex arrived a little later. Jip and Alex discussed the day's action, they talked well into the night. By the time Jip and Luci left it was past mid-night, and the pair were exhausted and they headed straight to their bus.

Casy and John meanwhile had been at the squat; they were shoring up a scaffolding tower, which they were to use as a look out post. As John was tightening the last bolt, Casy and Joe were fixing a video camera to the top.

"We have a wicked view!" Joe said as the first of the images started to appear on the monitor.

It was an image of a police van, which was disappearing over the hills.

From that time it was a quiet night at the squat.

The next morning was an early affair for the people who had stayed over night at the squat; everyone was woken up by the sound of lorries that were sounding their horns in a victorious way.

"Don't panic! They are only trying to intimidate us!" John reassured everyone as he was putting the kettle on.

Jip and Luci did not wake until Judy woke them. By the time they had arrived at the squat, the contractors had erected a giant steel solid fence that stretched for about half a mile! Jip was astounded by the quickness of it all.

When they entered the squat, John came running up to them and he told them all about the events of the morning.

Jip was not to pleased at what he heard and he stated that he and Luci would return to the site office and that if he was needed, anyone could contact him on his mobile phone.The pair of them headed off to the site office, once they had arrived there.

They found Suzie and Judy working hard, they were putting all of the completed petitions into a big black box,

"These are to go to Downing Street!" Judy said pointing at the box.

Luci was excited at the prospect of going to London with Jip. She expressed that she would contact the television crews and the media.

She stated that they were to leave that very day!
Jip told her sternly that they would not be leaving until everything was organised.
"A couple of days!" He said.
Luci looked despondent and she bowed her head. Jip saw this and he said,
"Luci, if we contact Steven in London, then he will arrange a meeting with us, then he would be able to bring all of his friends, we could walk to London with a demonstration!"
Luci accepted the explanation and she handed the mobile telephone to him, he looked at her, and Suzie butted in saying,
"We could do that Luci!"
Jip stroked Luci's hair and he gave her a kiss on the cheek.
"I have to tie a few things up first," Jip said as he left the site office in a kind of hurry.
Jip ran over to where there was a congregation of benders, there he saw Kirsten who was eating her breakfast. Jip asked her if she would be kind enough to help in the office as Jip knew she had a lot of friends in London. Kirsten agreed happily as she had nothing really planned and it would mean that she could talk with her friends for free.
Jip then headed off towards the tree house section and he went to where Kate had built her home.
He asked her the same question and she willingly obliged.
He then walked back across the Hill to the site office, as he passed by the café he was apprehended by a television crew,
"Is that thing on?" He asked.
He was told it was not yet! The man told Jip that Valleydale had gained international interest! He asked if his company could do a daily bulletin, which would be screened later that year. Jip agreed and he quickly ran off to the site office.When he had reached the site office, he slammed the door closed behind him.

He grabbed a pen and a piece of paper and he started to write, 'Mouths closed, ears open.'
He then pinned the note onto the notice board. Kissing Luci he then said that he would be back soon and he left again.
Jip jumped into the LandRover and he drove back to the squat, he met up with John and Casy who showed him the video surveillance camera and sound monitors that they had installed.
"Wicked!" Jip said.
John then told Jip that Alex had popped in and had left him a note. John then went and fetched the note and he placed it into Jip's hand.

CHAPTER EIGHT
LONDON CALLING

The days had passed by quietly; nobody was causing any trouble to anyone else. The people of the Hill were all busy preparing for the save the studio action. They knew that it would happen sooner than later.

Today was the planned action in London, everyone was asked to meet in Hyde Park for two o'clock.

This had meant that Jip and Luci with the petition box, had left earlier, it was so, they could have a bit of time in London before the start of the demonstration.

It had taken Jip about three hours on his motorcycle to reach London. The first place that Jip rode to was Brixton. They visited a squatted church there. The church had been set up over ten years ago; it was still alive and kicking! When they arrived, Luci spotted some of her old friends and she went and became busy discussing the old days with them. Jip went to the office where he saw Jan; they discussed the final delivery of the petition box.

"Quick! Pigs out front!" Someone shouted!

Jip panicked a bit and he fled carrying the petition box. He ran to the side entrance to where he had parked the motorcycle. As he was starting the engine, Luci joined him. Jip rode out the back way with Luci holding the box close to her tummy. They were soon doing sixty miles per hour along Brixton High Street. They headed for Kentish Town, Jip knew that the Rainbow Circle had squatted an old church too.

As they arrived, Jip noticed some really straight looking cars, which were brand new! He thought that this was really odd. Then he caught sight of Nikki; He had known her for a few years.

She stared at him and she shook her head! Jip understood this to be a go away kind of look. He nodded his head and rode away.

He decided that it might be safer to ride to Seven Kings.

At Seven Kings was Jip's old friend Ian, but to his dismay, when they reached his house, he was not there!

"What do we do now? I am sick of riding and this box is heavy!" Luci said as she dismounted and placed the box onto the floor.

Jip pointed to across the busy main road. Luci followed his finger, in her view she saw a public house.

Jip made his way over the road and he had to wait a bit as Luci had to wait for the traffic lights to show red,before her and the box could cross.

Once they were again together, they entered the pub. Ian was sat in a corner with his girlfriend; large bikers all wearing leather jackets surrounded him. A friendly greeting was had and a lot of introducing went on. Conversation was rife; Jip and Luci were offered an escort from the bikers. Jip accepted. After they had all finished their drinks they headed off.

There were ten motorcycles and they were descending on Hyde Park. The journey took them about twenty minutes. Jip enjoyed the challenge of riding his motorcycle with the others.

When they had arrived at Hyde Park, Ian led the bikers to just inside of the main gates. Every one of them was amazed at the sheer volume of people, lorries that were there to support the Hill! The atmosphere was electric. Jip looked around and all he saw was people smiling and he could hear laughter!

"You're a long way from home?" A voice said to him.

"So are you!" Jip said as he turned to see an old school mate.

Gary was a school chum and the pair had quite a natter about school days. After, Jip went to see Luci, she was sat on the first of the lorries, and she handed out flyers that had been made. It was then that Jip caught sight of kerrain. She was the contact for Downing Street.

"Hi! Darlings, are you set and ready?" She said as she met Jip.

The conversation flowed and Jip learnt that the secretary of State, Sir Alan Fellow would personally receive the petition from him, but only from behind the closed gates of Downing Street!

THE OTHER SIDE OF THE LINE

He was then told that the television companies were to screen the presentation live, when it happened.
The tabloid press had been informed and there was speculation that there was to be a great number of them present.
"It sounds organised enough to me!" Luci said as she was becoming rather excited.
Jip agreed and he walked over to where the bikers were all stood with their bikes. He asked them if they would escort him to the gates. After a little debate they agreed.
The stage was set. Jip decided that it was about time to speak to everyone. He climbed onto a lorry. His friends had made a stage area on the back. This was where Jip went and he picked up a microphone. He blew down it and cleared his throat.
"Good afternoon you right on people! The petition box has already tried to be confiscated, so please be wary! If you do experience any hostilities then feel free to telephone LIB. The number will be on the flyers" Jip finished his sentence and he looked about.
He then continued telling the people the ifs and why's, he ended saying,
"Let us go and deliver our pledge of peace!"
After he had spoke, the lorry he was stood on, it began to move slowly away. Other lorries and bikes followed. Behind there were around five thousand people, each carrying a flag or banner?
"Everyone has a place in their hearts for the Hill!" Luci said as the demonstration turned into The Mall.
It was clear to see that the police were very concerned about this action. There were constables everywhere dressed in riot gear!
"Something is wrong!" Jip said to himself.
As he finished philosophising.
The lorry that was carrying him suddenly came to a halt!
Jip looked and he saw that every policeman had a menacing look in his face.
'This is for humanity for life!' Jip thought.

68

THE OTHER SIDE OF THE LINE

In front of the lorry were two police Horses, they had forced the lorry to stop. Suddenly without warning one of the Horses bolted! It threw the rider helplessly to the floor! Jip rushed to see if the man had any injuries,

"Piss off hippie!" The policeman said as he dusted his tunic down.

Jip turned away in disgust and was immediately apprehended by a television crew who asked,

"We saw a policeman fall from his Horse! Did you see what happened?"

Jip could only be honest and he gave a detailed account of what he had seen. Just then, Kerrain waved her arms and shouted for Jip to

join her. This was perfect timing for Jip and he hastily headed to where Kerrain was stood with Luci. Luci had the petition box tightly in her arms and the bikers surrounded them.

"Let's go Jip!" Kerrain said as he joined her.

Luci grabbed Jip by the arm and the three of them all linked arms. They walked towards the big black gates.At the gate, they stood and waited. From the door of number eleven, a man walked out wearing a grey pinstriped suit. About thirty police officers dressed in riot gear surrounded him.

"Here we go!" Jip said to Luci.

The man, who was Sir Alan fellow, approached and as he did, so the police officers did. Jip reached for his crystal.

69

THE OTHER SIDE OF THE LINE

THE OTHER SIDE OF THE LINE

It was in his pocket, he tightly held it. Then there was total mayhem as the jostling started amongst the photographers and the television crews. They asked questions like,
"Did you have a safe journey?" To "Good afternoon secretary"
The secretary reached the gate and he spoke first,
"Good afternoon, I believe you have something of interest for me?"
"We have here a petition, it supports Valleydale's fight to stop section 48 from taking place on Hitchers Hill!" Jip said trying to be respectful.
"I take it, that there is an address where I can contact you good people?" The secretary said.
Jip felt a surge of frustration run the length of his body!
"I will give this a debate as soon as I am able! Thank you for bringing this to my attention" He continued.
The secretary then turned and walked back from where he had came from, the press was still asking questions as he entered number eleven. Jip and Luci tried to slip away quietly, but they were followed by a herd of reporters and photographers!

THE OTHER SIDE OF THE LINE

The questions rained from every angle, all that they could do was answer as many honestly.
Then there was an enormous rasp that rang in the air!
"It's tear gas!" A reporter shouted loudly.
Jip and Luci turned to run, as they did, they saw hundreds of riot police officers running at the crowds wielding their batons in a frightening manner!
Jip and Luci started to run for their lives! They saw friends being kicked and hit with the batons!
Jip even saw Nikki being dragged by her hair towards a riot van!
"Are you getting any of this?" Jip said to one of the reporters.
Most of them were running alongside Jip and Luci.
Before the reporter replied, Jip saw a policeman in riot gear walk up to his friend's lorry and smash the front windscreen!
Jip could not believe his eyes!
It was the sheer brutality that caught his attention most! It was all coming from the police!

72

THE OTHER SIDE OF THE LINE

Jip noticed a television camera that was perched on a brave mans shoulder. He ran so that he was in front of the Lens,
"It is pure police brutality! We are peaceful people who are non-violent!" He shouted.
The cameraman recorded Jip and then placed the camera under his arm and fled as fast as he could go!
Jip then realised that they were in the middle of a one sided battle. He was shocked!
It was then that their battle was over as a car had ploughed its way through the people to where Jip and Luci were running. The driver beckoned them in and they willingly did that!
The car reversed, trying to find a way out; but every exit was blocked with rows of riot police on Horses!
Jip and Luci were dropped on the nearest corner and they ran to the nearest bar!
When they sat down in the bar, all they could hear was the sound of police sirens and as they gazed around the air was filled with a sea of blue flashing light!

73

Then suddenly! The window at the front came crashing through! About thirty or so people staggered into the bar through the broken glass! One of them said,
"The police! They pushed us through!"
Jip stared at the barmaid; she went over to him and said,
"You can use the back entrance if you like?"
"Come on Luci, lets get the hell out of here!"
Jip said taking the barmaids offer.
The barmaid showed them the route.
Once out in the back street, Jip decided that it would be best if they hid somewhere for a while. They saw a low wall and climbed over it! Inside they saw a small garden shed.
"Perfect!" Jip said as they entered.
Luci complained that she had hurt her arm,
Jip told her that it was only a graze, as it was! The two huddled up in a corner.
Two hours lapsed by the time they decided to make their move. Jip had discovered an alleyway that led beside the houses to the next street. He had discussed the plan of action with Luci and they set off!
"Hey! What are you doing in my shed!" A man shouted as they emerged.
Neither Jip nor Luci said a word; they ran as fast as they could down the alley and away! Before they had realised how far they had ran, they found themselves in or near to Soho!
Jip checked his pocket. Once he had satisfied himself that he had enough money, he took Luci to the nearest restaurant.
Once sat and drinking a glass of wine, Jip started realising what actually had happened, his mind was visualising the whole event!
Jip came to an honest conclusion. He was sure that none of the looting was done by any of the people who he had seen. He knew what kind of people they were, peaceful people!
"Luci have you heard of the B.N.K?" He asked her..
Luci shook her head as she had a mouthful of food at that moment.

THE OTHER SIDE OF THE LINE

"They are here! They are causing violence and disrupted behaviour amongst normal peace loving people!" Jip said.

Jip then went into a deep conversation of how the B.N.K movement was Government funded. The moles were sent to turn the key one might say.

Luci found it all a touch much and she was sceptical, the truth being that she did not want to believe what she was hearing.

"Something has to be done?" Jip finished saying.

Then suddenly his mobile telephone sprang to life; jumping, he was very nervous!

He had a discussion with Judy who was at the Hill. Apparently, the event was shown live on the television. The police had read out a statement that blamed the organisers! Jip's name was mentioned!

Judy asked him if he could get back to the Hill as soon as they could, she said that she suspected happenings at the squat! Jip did not like the feeling he had at all!

THE OTHER SIDE OF THE LINE

When the conversation was over, he paid the bill while Luci used the woman's room. All done, they went to find a taxi rank, they saw one on the corner. Jip asked the driver if he could take them to Paddington Station.
The driver talked of the riots! Jip felt tense as they approached the station. Luci saw a couple of policemen, then some more! Jip asked the driver if he could drop them a little further down the road.
The driver asked him,
"Are you a dodger?"
Jip was not happy! He ordered the driver to stop the black cab! He shoved a twenty-pound note in the driver's hand and left the cab. Luci waited for the change and then caught up to him.
"What now?" She said as she grabbed his arm.
Jip stated that he did not think it would be a god idea to catch a train. He opted for a bus instead. They were lucky as the bus they were hunting was actually at the stop!
"What a stroke of luck!" He said to Luci.
The bus was soon moving; they headed towards north London. Jip was going to his old friends George's house.
The bus stopped about thirty yards from his house. Once they had received an answer from George at his front door, they were invited to use his spare room. George was just heading for his bed as he had came to the end of his shift at work.
He worked on the oil- rigs doing one month on and one month off; he had just served a month.
Jip and Luci slept soundly, but Luci did wake a few times and she stared at the ceiling.

THE OTHER SIDE OF THE LINE

CHAPTER NINE

In Valleydale, the squat was still occupied and the Hill was still teaming with people. The sun was out and all around you could see children playing their games.

Judy was in the site office as usual, this morning she had been joined by John and Suzie; they were concerned about the London affair. The telephone did not ring or the fax did not receive. John thought it odd, so he started to play his flute.

"That is really beautiful" Judy declares as she looked at her watch.

"Give it an hour and I will telephone Jip" She said.

John stopped playing and agreed while Suzie nodded her head in approval. At 27 Balls pond road, London north one. George asked Jip if he had any change, this was so he could go and get some milk. Jip gave him a ten-pound note and asked if he would be kind enough to fetch every Newspaper that was in the shop. He hinted that he did not mean it literally! George smiled and he made his way out, the shop, was only two doors away. It was just as he left that he saw Luci walking down the stairs, he asked if she needed anything from the shop and she answered quite close to Jip's statement. George shook his head and closed the door behind him.

Luci went to find Jip; he was in the kitchen buttering her toast.

"Worried?" Luci said as she kissed Jip.

"Yea, are you?" Jip replied.

Luci said that she was petrified, yet she felt a strange sense of positivity inside of her body. Jip kissed her again and as they were cuddling, George walked in carrying a bundle of Newspapers in his arms. Hanging from his pocket rather precariously was a pint of milk.

"I will not read any of those until I have drank my coffee!" Jip stated as he prepared three cups of coffee.

Luci did not wait and after she had retrieved them from George. She said excitedly,

"Jip our picture is in every paper!"

George laughed loudly; it was all a bit much for him, as it was his first day off for a month. Jip then finished his coffee and began to read the first paper. The headlines read,

HARSH REALITY AS POLICE CHARGE PROTESTERS

THE DAILEY PLONTIN
Story by Emanuel Disbar

Scenes of violence erupted last night after a would be peaceful protest went dreadfully wrong. Around 200 arrests and 100 injured as police some say wrongly waded into the protesters. The statement from the police read to a live audience was that of pure dictatorship, quote,
A police officer was knocked from his Horse and abuse was being thrown at them so it was decided to end the demonstration abruptly.
Live television cameras witnessed the handing over of a petition and as they were setting the equipment up pictures were recorded and if the film is slowed down. It clearly showed the Horse rear, as it's front legs slipped on a manhole cover. It was plain to see that the police action was, as said by a spokesperson known as Jip, Quote,
"This is sheer police brutality to peaceful people!"
This peaceful protest had been set up to illustrate the danger of section 48 being made a reality. Section 48 was mentioned in the arms reduction deal that was placed into force this year.
Every environmental group in the world fiercely fights the policy. A representative for the Foot co-operation was quoted stating,
"The policy is ludicrous! It is dangerous and any mistake could cost lives!"
We take an in-depth look at section 48 on pages 9,10, and 11. Police would like to speak with Jip and his female companion, this would be to eliminate them from their enquiries.

THE DAY A PEACEFUL, GOOD INTENTION WENT TERRIBLY WRONG!

After the Claremont road protest, where an 82 year old woman was forced to leave her life long home, were the police properly briefed in their activities?
Are the protesters really a menace to society when all they care for is the environment?
Are the protesters a breed of unwashed poverty stricken people?
Will the government look more closely at section 48 after this broadly published protest?
Will they re-open the case of section 48 and Valleydale?
Yesterday was a day the politicians say was a reminder of the 1930's. A day when the police were delivering their pledge of law and order, the protesters were only exercising their legal right to protest and the bloody battle was one that had been seen once before. Our question is? Was it protest or was it a riot!
Jip then read on,
Jip was shocked as he read the last sentence,
"Luci the police want to question us!" He said being really serious.
Luci stated that she could not cope with seeing them at that moment and she told him that she felt scared.George was listening and he walked over to his jacket, which was hanging from the door. Out of the pocket he pulled a set of keys.
"My wheels are out back, I can take you anywhere that you want to go!" He said grinning.
Jip deliberated for a while and he finally came with the decision,
"Valleydale would be great if you don't mind?" Jip said.
George said that he fancied a trip into the country and as he had always loved Wales, then it would be perfect for him.That settled, and they all went about their early morning duties. Jip went to the bathroom and as he was washing his face he heard his mobile telephone ringing in the kitchen. Luci answered it and he heard her start chatting. Jip stared into the mirror, he thought that he was looking ragged, he had three days growth of hair on his chin. Luci knocked on the door and she entered and handed him the telephone.

It was Judy who was telephoning from the Hill! Jip was then in a deep conversation about the newspapers and the police,
"Listen Judy, let us think about saving our Hill!" He said then turned the telephone off.
Luci then went back downstairs and she shouted that George was ready to leave. Jip dried himself and put his shirt back on and he was soon with the others.
"You will like this one?" George said as he guided them to his garage. Inside was a gorgeous 1968 Ford Zodiac! It was customised and Jip loved the purple bodywork and the alloy wheels.
Jip saw the size of the exhaust and he stated,
"Is it a V-8?" He was talking about the size of the engine capacity.
George smiled and they all jumped into the car.
"This is comfortable George!" Luci said as George started reversing.
"Bloody pain these blackened out windows!" George laughed.
It was not very long and they were cruising on the motorway, the cassette player was playing some reggae. Jip felt relief at leaving London. George was enjoying driving his beloved motor car. Luci then remembered the newspapers and she started to read them, Jip fell into his peaceful thinking mode as they winged their way to the Hill.
Back at the Hill, there was a lot of confusion going on. Around 8 uniformed police officers were arresting John; they had turned up telling John that they had a warrant for his arrest! John only had an outstanding court case and could not understand why! The police told him that they would be able to sort the muddle out back at the police station. John did not fancy that so when Casy came trotting up with his Horse, John made his getaway! It must have been funny as the Horse decided to drop his load right at the correct time, it made the officer's scramble away, and so John was able to run onto the Hill and disappear! The police were then left red faced as the people of the Hill started to sing and dance all around them! John laughed as he watched from Casy's tree house. He saw when the police drove the van away and he could see it right down the valley.

THE OTHER SIDE OF THE LINE

He watched as it pulled up at the end of the lane.
"They are probably waiting for Jip and Luci!" Casy said to John when the fuss had died down. John thought that it might be a good idea to telephone Jip and let him know about the situation.
Casy rode off to the office to fetch one of the mobile telephones.
At the site office and Jip's bus, was total confusion as a set of people was making the entrance into a gate.
They had made the gate by cutting an old car in two and placing each half on either side, then they used some scaffolding poles with wood brightly painted. To Casy it was a piece of art!
Casy went to the cupboard and picked out a telephone. He galloped as fast as he could back to where John was hiding in his tree house. The telephone was soon in John's hands. He telephoned Jip and told him of the police activity.

THE OTHER SIDE OF THE LINE

Jip said that he suspected the police mistook John as Him! Jip then, explained that the car they were travelling in had black windows and it would be impossible to see through them from a distance. John felt relieved and he thought he would go and greet them, in his mind was that if the police saw Jip, then he would be able to take there attention from him. It was John's secret plan!

Inside the car a dilemma was growing, Jip was worrying because he saw that they were implicated in causing a riot! Luci admitted that she was scared again, Jip told her that they had to be strong and that it would be ok when they returned to the Hill. Luci accepted and she went back to reading.

"Is it this turning Jip?" George asked.

Jip then instructed George that it was the turning. Not long afterwards and they had entered Valleydale, Jip telephoned the site office and everyone became excited.

"The hero's are returning home!" Judy shouted after she had taken the call.

Inside the car it was a nervous affair as they turned to cross the bridge. As the car turned, George whispered to Jip that the police were on the side of the road! He asked if they should just drive on or should they turn around? Jip asked George to go like a rocket past the police van. George pushed his foot hard onto the accelerator pedal and they zoomed past the police. they seemed more interested in looking at the car than its occupants! This was good for them all that was until they spotted John! Jip felt paranoid as George picked him up and he thrashed the car to the top. He had to brake severely at the top as the new gate was closed! It was John who leapt out and he opened it and closed it when they had entered.

"We are home at last!" Luci said as she entered the bus.

The greeting for Jip was very subdued, as no one really knew what state of mind he would be in. Jip was tired and he told everyone that he would speak with him or her in the morning. That was it then for the day as Jip and Luci went to their bed in the bus.

THE OTHER SIDE OF THE LINE

George wondered around the site, that was until he was tired and he slept in his car.The next morning Jip was awoken quite early by the sound of motorcycle engines. He had to fumble his way to the door, as he could not wake that morning.

When Jip finally answered the knock on the door, he was surprised to see Dave the biker. Dave gave Jip his bike keys and he said,

"Back without a scratch, it rides well!"

Jip was pleased that Dave had rode his B.S.A back from London and that it was now safely parked behind the bus. That was it for the day! Dave had brought a couple of bottles of cider and there was no coffee that morning. It did not take long and Jip's bus was chocker-block with people all asking him of his exploits in London! Luci arrived from the bed a little later and she found Jip half cut from drinking. She thought if you could not beat them then join them! She had a bottle of Martini that she opened and shared with the other girls who were there. The evening seemed quickly to arrive and everyone was a little worse for wear when Judy came running in, she had to scream so everyone turned his or her attentions to her!

"Quick! They are trying to get the squat!" She cried out.

There was pandemonium as everyone ran or staggered down the Hill to the squat!

Just as Jip arrived and reached the back door, he saw rows of police officers all across the road out the front of the squatted studio. A large fat police officer was holding a megaphone,

"This is Government property! I have a warrant that states you must vacate this property by 12 o'clock midnight tonight!" The policeman shouted through the megaphone.

The police officer watched as people started to climb onto the roof of the studio, they were tying themselves to the chimney, and a couple of them strapped their hands onto the guttering.

"We are not moving! Not until we have spoken with the minister in charge of you lot!" John shouted from a top window.

The police officer heard this and he just turned around and retreated.

Straight back to one of the numerous police vans that were there. The people who had fastened themselves to the roof stayed there! John waited in the window. Jip was checking that everyone was all right, the truth was that most were ill and feeling the effects of the alcohol that they had drank earlier in the day, and some were still drinking! Everything was then quiet and an air of tension rose between the conflicting parties.

"This is only the start," Jip said to the people who were near him.

Jip was not very often wrong.

It was 11:30pm when the conflict happened.

The police move was to say the least very cruel, around sixty or so officers went charging in though the front door and they were not in a playing mood! Jip realised this and he ran for the back door, but as he fumbled trying to find the right key, he was rushed by about ten policemen. He was dragged onto the floor and he was kicked and punched by the officers who were shouting things like,

"We are not your minions! You are fucking Hippies! Take that you scum!"

Jip lost consciousness and he was carried and slapped into the back of a police van. He came around to see John opposite him; John was covered in blood!

"You alright John?" Jip asked.

"The bastards they came upstairs and they cut them down from the roof! Then they threw me down the stairs!" John replied in a state of shock.

"They rushed me!" Jip told John.

"It's too much!" John said, as he was obviously feeling sorry for himself.

John lay down and as he did he yelled out a cry of pain. He was not pretending as he had broken his shoulder!

Jip spat blood onto the floor, then as he started to study it; the rear door opened and in flew Dave and two of his friends. Dave was kicking and screamed,

THE OTHER SIDE OF THE LINE

"Bastards! I will have you!"
"Dave let it go!" Jip shouted to him, as the rear door was slammed closed.
Then the unexplained happened! The van started to move in a quick fashion, all the occupants could here were shouts of,
"Stop that van, get him before he escapes"
Then the shouting grew dim and Jip and the others were surprised when the hatch that separates the prisoners from the driver opened. Casy's eyes appeared and he said,
"Are you alright chaps!"
"How?" Was all Jip could say as he was not sure whether he was glad or not.
Casy shouted that he saw the van unattended and he borrowed it!
He then winked and said,
"Get ready we are entering the Hill!"
Then before they had time to speak, Casy had stopped the van and opened the back doors. Jip was dazed and he staggered into the waiting Luci's arms. He asked for her to fetch the pair of bolt cutters from the bus. He showed the handcuffs that they all were wearing. It did not take very long and everyone's handcuffs were twisted metals that they threw onto Casy's scrap pile!

Luci took Jip onto the bus and she started to tend his wounds, he had a cut lip and a few little cuts to his head. His elbows and arms were full of scrapes.Neither of them noticed when Dave and his friends drove the police van to just outside of the barrier, they parked it so that it straddled the road blocking it!
Dave then poured petrol all over it.
Soon the sky was alight with the silhouette of the flames!
The police were so busy arresting the members of the squat that they failed to notice the van burning.
By the day break the next morning all that was left was a burnt out shell of what once was a piece of Government property. John had his arm in a sling and was talking in the site office with Jip. They were discussing the last evening's events when the mobile telephone number that they had issued on the petition sheet began to ring! Jip sat and let it ring, as he became very worried. John prompted him after a while to answer it by given him a stern look. Jip took note and answered it. The reply was to astound everyone everywhere!
The Secretary of state himself telephoned the number!
He spoke to Jip as if he knew him well; he told Jip that after careful consideration he had decided to review the policy of section 48.
That meant that once the tunnel had been sealed then work would stop until after the review had taken place!
"I am very relieved to hear this" Jip said.
The two then passed complimentary passing comments and the call was terminated. Jip did not say a word as he was coming to terms with the ease that the news had brought. John realised, it was something important and he went and fetched Luci and Suzie. Judy saw them, and followed when John gave her the nod.
As soon as they reached the site office, Jip saw Luci and he went to her and held her hands and he said,
"They are reviewing section 48! Yip!"
John fell back with a giant grin on his face and everyone danced excitedly,

THE OTHER SIDE OF THE LINE

"Party at the Hill tonight!" Luci shouted with tears of joy streaming down her face.

Jip then asked everyone if they would round up who was left to attend the site office in an hour's time.

It was quite funny to see as the news travelled so fast, all you saw was people running and jumping with joy as each heard the news.

Jip was then passed the local evening paper; he nearly fainted when he read,

  HILL GETS A REPRIEVE!

Jip then turned the page to see another headline that read,

 HOORAY FOR THE HILL

Everything was happening at a very fast pace and all around where Jip was stood the people were all full of joy and happiness! That made Jip feel good until he turned to the next page!

Looming in front of his eyes, was a picture of him and Luci at the demonstration in London, it began,

GIVE YOURSELVES UP!

Jip was shattered as he read the article; he walked over to where a little tree stump was sprouting from the ground.

He sat on the stump and placed his hands to his head and he repeated a lot of swear words to himself!

Casy noticed Jip and he went over and he joined him, John followed Casy. They both knew that this could only be the beginning! The pair sat with Jip and they discussed their next move.

88

John expressed his worry about being banged up; Casy was adamant that the police would not send them to court. Jip decided that he would not hand himself over as he felt he had done no wrong. They all agreed to carry on as they were until further notice!

Back in the site office caravan Luci had gone back to finish opening the large amount of mail. This she enjoyed doing and her joy turned into estactic excitement when she discovered eight tickets to Egypt, from Sarah H! Luci ran leaping as she went over to where the boys were all sat,

"Jip look! Eight! Eight tickets to Egypt from Sarah!" She excitedly babbled out.

Jip's first thoughts were of a spiritual nature as he thought the tickets were meant as a proverb. But then he came to his normal senses and he said,"Please don't get over excited everyone, how could we possibly leave for Egypt, we have so much to do here and the bleeding law want us!"

The smiling all turned into anguished looks, that was until Luci said, "Well let us celebrate the great news anyway!" Luci said changing the subject.

"Yes a party would be very fitting!" Elaine said as she joined them.

Luci had watched Elaine pull up in her car and she saw her grab the paper before she stepped out. She came trotting over showing the front cover of the newspaper and she was smiling. It was a happy greeting and Elaine promised that she had a crate of lager in the trunk of her car. As she and a male helper went to fetch the beer. Jip and John both went and fetched their musical instruments. Jip was last as usual and after splitting open a can of lager he played an E chord and he started to sing,

THE OTHER SIDE OF THE LINE

The games are yet to come alive
As each pawn still fights to survive
We all have tried to live and be peaceful
We have learnt that if we try we can be fruitful

So bring in the peace
Let in the love
Show us some faith
Save the trees
Keep the valleys green and the water flowing
Watch as the creations are growing

We just don't want to play
In playgrounds for the rich
We care for everyone
We care for anyone
We really care for you
We do care it really is true

Bring in the peace
Bring in the love
Feel the tree
Let us learn to live and be free

John then stopped playing his flute and he started to tap the ground with a stick that he had found near to him, John also began to sing,

It is now, the time to party
So come on and have some fun
Let the talk be started and let everyone know we have won
This is ours, stage one, stage one

Once the song finally ended, Jip noticed a large number of people had arrived at the gate and were entering the Hill. As the people became closer their noise level was high! They were shouting things like, "Yip! We have won" or "Hooray we are free!"
Jip saw that it was in fact the people who had been arrested at the squat, everywhere around was Joy! Casy saw Suzie and ran to her and he planted a giant kiss onto her lips.
"We are lucky, I guess! They let us all go after they had cautioned us, they were not very apologetic though!" Suzie said as she withdrew from Casy's tight grip.
"So did they arrest anyone for squatting?" Jip asked Kim.
Kim was a very quiet man; Jip had met him quite a few years previous when they both were drinkers.
"They kept asking us about you boys, they mentioned something of criminal damage!" Kim replied.
Jip said that he thought they would throw the book at them. This somehow caused everyone to burst out in simultaneous laughter! The party was then well under way and the drinking and smoking raved well into the night.
When the party was at the High spot, nearly the whole of the village had turned up all in great cheer! It was daylight before most of the population of the Hill had any sleep. Jip and Luci retired to the bus as Casy and John went to their tree houses.

CHAPTER TEN

The next day John woke as everyone else, it was about 2 o'clock in the afternoon. He was in extreme pain with his shoulder, he decided that he would need hospital attention, Dave took him on Jip's motorcycle to the nearest city, which was Cardiff. John had fun trying to hold on with his best arm as Dave rushed to the hospital. They were soon there. John was actually seen quiet quickly and the doctors fixed his shoulder in an efficient way. John fancied the nurse and he spent most of the time talking with her.
"Come on Casanova!" Dave said.
"Just because you have not the touch dear fellow!" John said taking the Mickey slightly!
John then started to struggle to put the crash helmet over his head, the nurse gave him a hand, and he blew her a kiss from inside the helmet once it was tightly in place. They were soon zooming out of the hospital grounds and heading back to the Hill. John was a little more comfortable as they roared along.
As soon as they had turned off of the motorway, Dave noticed a bus parked in a lay-by, it was advertising breakfasts. Dave thought of his stomach and he pulled in, John was concerned that the café bus might not have a vegetarian menu.
Once they were on board they found out that it did sell vegetarian food! Dave also considered the price to be cheap! They ordered their breakfasts, John with his vegetarian, Dave had the big mans breakfast as it was called. They both drank coffee. There were newspapers handy and they both settled down to reading the paper and eating their breakfasts. They soon had become intense with reading.
They did not see two police officers pull up and look over the motorcycle! One of the officers had called on his radio for a personal number check when John first saw them. John found it hard to tell Dave in a quiet fashion as he was ignoring him while he ate his food.

THE OTHER SIDE OF THE LINE

THE OTHER SIDE OF THE LINE

When John finally got through to him, Dave told John to go and use the toilet. The toilet was situated in the lay-by; it was on the opposite side of the bus than where the bike was parked.

John did just that after the young assistant cook asked politely if they could leave as she did not need any trouble in the café bus.

Dave walked over to the motorcycle and he greeted the officers with, "I have borrowed it for the day!"

The two police officers turned and faced him, one of them said, "I recognise you! From the night at the squat! You escaped that time but you will not this time!"

The two officers lunged at Dave! He started fighting and one of the officers used his radio to request back up. John had already fled and when he thought he was well away he started to hitch hike. He had his crash helmet over his good arm as he stuck his thumb out. He slowly walked and after a minute or so, he heard a car slow behind him. He stopped and turned around only to see it was a police patrol car! The driver of the police car was another of the officers that was involved the night at the squat. John was devastated; he did not struggle as his arm was laid tightly across his chest.

The police car then headed back into Cardiff with John sat unhappily in the back seat. As they drove, John saw two other police cars that flew past them in the opposite direction. They had their blue lights flashing and their sirens wailing.

'Dave must be having fun!' John thought to himself and a snug smile caressed his lips.

It did not seem to be very long when they finally arrived at the police station. John was taken to meet the desk sergeant and was asked if he would like to telephone anyone.

"Yes, my girlfriend Judy" John replied.

The police sergeant then asked John for the telephone number. John in no uncertain words told him that he would not give him anything!

"Slap him in a cell" The sergeant aggressively said.

Just as John was settling into the cell.

He heard a commotion and listened at the door, it was Dave arriving.
"Stick him in with his mate, they are both bang to rights!" The sergeant shouted.
Dave then came flying through the cell door and he very closely missed John's bad shoulder as he did!
"Hey! Slow it down will you!" John shouted.
" I want a doctor and I need a drink! " Dave shouted.
Neither of them had a reply, all they saw was a weird looking officer slam the hatch closed.
That was all that the pair saw for the afternoon, it was nearly 4 hours later when they did finally get some result from shouting through the door. John was allowed his one and only telephone call and he was introduced to the duty solicitor. Dave saw the doctor and had a drink of water.. The duty solicitor contacted Mr P. P. Mcterry, who was John's personal solicitor.
Back at the Hill and it was early evening when Judy received the call. When she had finished the call she ran over to where Jip and Luci were on their bus. She informed them of the where about of Jip's motorcycle. Jip left the upset Judy to sit with Luci, he went to see Casy, and Casy took him over to Suzie. Suzie said that she would spread the word.
Jip then returned to his bus and on entering he asked,
"Who will take him some cigarette's?"
Jip said meaning John.
"I will! I need to see John!" Judy said biting the cherry.
George had arrived and after the discussion he offered to give Judy a lift to Cardiff police station. She accepted and they headed off in George's car.
Jip and Luci looked at each other, they knew each other so well that they did not have to speak to know what the other was thinking. Jip was panicking and so was Luci,
"Don't panic, we will go and have a holiday at my mums for a couple of days!" Jip told her.

THE OTHER SIDE OF THE LINE

Luci asked why they could not go to Egypt. Jip told her to think straight! They would not be able to leave the country legally at that particular time.

There was a knock on the door of the bus; Jip did not recognise the knock, so he personally answered it.

At the door he found Elaine with Alex and the pair looked to be cold. Jip invited them on board and Luci supplied them with hot tea.

Over tea, Jip said,

"I am afraid that we have had some bother down at the squat."

"I'm not too interested in that at the moment Jip. I have actually came by to personally urge you to give yourself up to the police and get this mess sorted!" Alex spoke passionately.

A deep and long conversation pursued and Alex left in a huff. Elaine was not happy! Jip followed the councillor out of the bus trying to speak to him. Alex went and sat on the log that was close to the bus. Jip joined him.

"I will not tell them what you have told me Jip" Alex thoughtfully said.

"Look Alex I don't want us to fall out" Jip said politely.

"No, nor I. It is not your fault, I see your side of things and I believe them to be true and factual, but, I am the local councillor. I am finding it hard to bring myself to decide which way I turn, the major contacted me last night. He demanded I spoke with you. He was afraid that Valleydale was getting the wrong kind of image!"

Jip asked him what he said to the major?

"I have had the police and the Masonic lodge contact me as well!" Alex replied a little surprised at Jip's formidable question.

"Well, what did you tell them Alex?" Jip was becoming intense.

Alex then told Jip that he had done Jip a favour, he stated that he knew Jip well and that he trusted him and that the matter in London could not possibly had been caused by his influence. He also stated that he did not agree with the accusations that were flying around. Alex then took his wallet from his pocket to gather a few cards.

Pictures of his children fell out, this made Jip think that Alex was still married and knocking off Elaine. Jip was pleased as Alex saw that Jip had realised his secret.
"Not a word?" Alex giggled into Jip's ear.
Jip then told Alex that he could inform the majoress etc. That him and Luci were to go away for a couple of days for a break as so much had happened, and he stated that he needed the time to think. Elaine then slowly glided over to where the men were sat. Jip used this as an excuse, and he said his goodbyes and left the two together.
Jip went over to the site office where he found Casy sat taking Judy's place while she was away visiting John. Jip astounded Casy when he grabbed a mobile telephone and he dialled the police!
It was funny, Jip explained his name, but the policeman on the receiving end did not know anything about him! Jip had to tell him that his name was splattered all over the evening's paper! The police officer asked Jip to wait. Then he asked him if he could dial another number that he would give to him,
Jip said,
"Look I am going away for a few days to sort out my head, when I return I will hand myself in ok!"
He turned the telephone off.
Casy stared at Jip with baited breath,
"What!" He said.
Jip winked at Casy and he left the site office, he was in a bit of a hurry, he thought that the police may know now, that they were at the Hill. When he returned to his bus he grabbed a bag with some things and Luci did the same. Jip went back to the site office and he took the LandRover keys,
"Back in a few days!" He said to Casy.
Soon Jip and Luci were in the LandRover and they were leaving the site.
"Where are we going love?" Luci asked.
"To the garage to fill this with diesel!" Jip replied.

CHAPTER ELEVEN

As the music blared away inside the LandRover, Jip having left the motorway in search of a café that would serve a vegetarian cuisine. They trundled along past an unseen traveller's site. Jip saw on a tree a poster that was advertising the plight of the Hill. To him it seemed to be in the middle of nowhere, he slowed the LandRover to a crawl, and he noticed a cottage that was high into the hillside. It had smoke billowing from the chimney. Jip then saw a tiny lane and he turned the vehicle into it. It was vary bumpy but the LandRover loved it! Once they reached the end of the lane they came across a fence which had a stile that they would have to climb over to get to the cottage. Both Jip and Luci did this and when they were over they saw metal bars, that were hanging purposely from a metal frame, Jip thought of Tubular Bells! Then they saw a drum, which had what looked like a buffalo skin on it.They approached the entrance to the cottage, as they did a funny looking old man came out of the door to greet them. The man looked like a professor! The one's you see on the television.
"Good afternoon, and to what delight do I owe this visit?" The grey haired man asked.
Jip explained that he had seen the poster and that they were from the Hill. He also could see a couple of posters in the upstairs windows of the cottage and he pointed to these.
"I see, you are that fellow they call Jip are you not?" The man said.
Jip nodded in a proud way.
"Well it is wonderful to meet such an upstanding character like yourself!" The man said smiling.
The conversation was rife and after a while the man offered them to enter his home, they accepted and as they entered Jip felt he had gone back in time.The cottage was full of very old musical instruments and the walls were covered with pictures of old blues musicians scanning decades!

In the corner of the downstairs room there was an inviting looking wood-burning stove, on the top was a quaint green coloured tea pot, the man asked if they would like some of his special herb tea. After a cup of tea, Jip asked if he might look at some of the instruments, the man handed him a Lute, which Jip started to play. After about an hour or so and they noticed that the night was creeping in. Jip said that they should leave, but the old man told them that if they wanted they could stay with him in the cottage. He said that he slept upstairs and they would be welcome to sleep in the living area downstairs. Jip discussed the idea with Luci and she was tired so she agreed.

The evening was spent drinking the man's; who name was Pat, homemade wine. They sat in front of a beautiful log fire sipping the wine which pat had mulled to perfection. It was at least midnight when Pat retired to his bed. Jip and Luci snuggled up near to the fire and they were soon peacefully asleep.

The next morning was an early one for them as a Cockerel started to screech at first light. Pat did not murmur. Jip and Luci helped themselves to a cup of tea and Luci wrote a thank you note inviting Pat to visit the Hill. As they left Jip picked up a stick and he played a small but melodic tune on the metal bars. Luci stated that she was hungry, so Jip rushed to the LandRover. He was feeling much happier today! They had to drive for a good ten miles until they came to a small village where they found a café; they were lucky as the café sold a vegetarian breakfast.

Jip saw a Newsagents shop opposite and he went and bought a map. He started reading it as they waited, for their breakfasts to be cooked. Luci stated that she saw a lorry that had Cornwall written on the side. Jip knew that Luci wanted to go there. He realised that the turning he had taken actually headed him for Salisbury!

"We will take the old road to Salisbury and then the A303 to Exeter if you like" He said to her.

Luci said that she was not fussed, and she asked if Stonehenge was on the way.

THE OTHER SIDE OF THE LINE

Jip said it was kind of and they decided that they would buy lunch in Salisbury and eat it a Stonehenge! Jip said that it would take about an hour to get to Salisbury. He stated that they had only just had breakfast. Luci laughed and told him that she needed to go to the Stones! Jip had to agree with her, as when she had a notion, if he did not play ball then his life would be hell!

Back on the Hill, George and Judy had returned late from the police station and were just waking up.

Judy had stayed in John's tree house. George was again sleeping in his car. Judy walked over to the site café and along her way she saw Suzie, who was lighting her fire. Judy went over to Judy and she explained when she was asked, about John and they talked for a few minutes. Judy ended up crying! As she thought, that John would have no chance of getting bailed from the court! She told Suzie that John and Dave were both in court that very morning! Suzie said that she would like to go along with her and they both headed up to the site office.

"Jes! Could you take care of my fire, I've just lit it!" Suzie asked.

Jes said she would and she wished them luck, she did know that John and Dave had been arrested, she took particular interest, as she kind of liked Dave!

Casy woke up and fed his Horses and he saw George who was heading to the site café, he went over and they both sat together drinking. their first of the morning drinks. They discussed the court appearances that were to happen that day. It was decided that a posy of people would attend. Casy would drive a van, while George would take the women in his car.. George did not argue!

So it was 10 o'clock in the morning when they were all set to leave for the courts. Casy was driving Jes's van, which was filled with people! George had Suzie and Judy in the car.

It was around this time that Jip and Luci were on the A303 heading to Salisbury, Luci had not long ago reminded Jip that she wanted to go to see Stonehenge.

THE OTHER SIDE OF THE LINE

Jip relayed the plan to her twice; she finally did understand what Jip was doing. They drove into Salisbury and they bought provisions for a vegetarian feast! On the journey to the Stones, Jip saw a couple who was hitch hiking and he instinctively pulled over and offered them a lift. Jip asked the male hitchhiker, if the Stones would be any use to them! The Hitchers said that they were heading for a free festival that was happening in Dorset and they urged Jip to go! Luci joined in saying,
" We are meant to be on holiday remember?"
Jip kept his thoughts to himself and he did not murmur a word until they reached the Stones.
Then all he said was,
"I will pull up the lane where the energy is best."

If you have ever seen Stonehenge then you might have noticed the lane that runs parallel to the Stones, you can stop there for a while! Jip, Luci, and the two hikers shared a lavish lunch.

Jip remarked on the fact that he was hungrier travelling than he was back at his bus. The discussion was then all about the free festival. Jip was rail roaded by Luci into accepting to go to the event!
"Only for one night!" Jip said.
Luci then cleaned up all of the debris they had caused and Jip studied the map. The male hiker helped Jip plan a route, and soon they were back driving again. Jip decided that if they saw a shop that sold beer then he would buy a crate and sell the cans for one pound each! That was what he told Luci, but it was really an excuse!
Back in Cardiff, John and Dave had been hauled up in front of the magistrates, John's solicitor was smart, and after a while the verdict was announced. John was bailed to appear again in 3 weeks time!
The reason given was, so that he could attend the hospital and fix his shoulder! Dave was remanded!
He had stood earily staring at the judge while the judge read out his verdict.
There was uproar as Dave jumped out of the box and he ran for the door, it was not a very good plan, as in the doorway was stood about six police officers! Dave ran back into the courtroom and it was funny as he growled at the judge just as he was bowled over by the policemen.
Judy who was watching with the others shook her head in disgust! She ran to John and hugged him tightly. All John shouted was,
"Judy! Watch my arm!"
It was not long, before they were outside and Television crews were waiting.
John was mainly asked about the whereabouts of Jip and his female companion.
John said that they would be handing themselves over to the police when they had returned from a family crisis that they were attending! It seemed a good excuse John thought to himself. Then all the people, plus John left and went back to the Hill.

THE OTHER SIDE OF THE LINE

Poor Dave was slammed back into the dingy smelly cells that are at most courts. It is a disgrace! Was Dave's thinking?
Things were becoming rather nerves racking for Jip and Luci. They had arrived at the entrance to the festival! They were in a queue and the police was looking at every car that was in front, as it entered the site! Then like magic! An old friend of Jip's saw him. He was working as a steward at the gate.
"Let me drive and I will take you over to the back stage area, away from all of this!"
Jip crammed up tight to Luci. The friend in his bright orange dayglow smock turned the LandRover around He drove about a mile, to another entrance; this was the artist's entrance.
Before long, Jip and Luci were enjoying the company of a few singers and musicians that had played at the Hill.
They were offered a caravan to stay in and they accepted. The hikers had left to see their friends and they had promised to visit the Hill.
Jip and Luci took their bags and sat in the caravan, Jip was asked if he would play that evening with the band and he agreed.
Back at the Hill. John sat with Judy quietly staring out over the Hill. It was very peaceful and as they looked about all that they saw was beautiful people, all sitting peacefully by their open fires. It felt as if you would be able to sit and energise yourself with the vibe of the Hill.
It would be a dream for any city dweller.

CHAPTER TWELVE

It was Monday morning. The sun was shining; Jip and Luci were waving goodbye to their friends. The festival was still well alive, Jip and Luci though, were 3 days late to hand themselves over to the police. It was decided after a deep discussion was had, that they would go and tell the truth to the police. Jip had the impression that he had done no wrong, so what could they actually do to him? Luci stated that she was very scared of being locked away. Jip told her that it would not happen and she seemed to go on his word. They were heading towards Cardiff and Valleydale. Once they had joined the motorway, Jip was sure that a white car was following him. Luci watched and she told him that the car had been following for the last ten minutes!

"Well that's it!" Luci said feeling as if she had been caught for something.

Jip explained that he was sure this was only an escort back to the Hill. He told Luci that he thought they would follow him all of the way! Luci liked what she heard and she again relaxed.

They had been travelling for two hours and Jip said he needed a drink. Luci grabbed the map and she instructed Jip to take an early turn from the motorway,

"We can go back via Newport this way!" She said.

Jip did not bother to look at the map, as he could trust Luci's directions. Just!

Soon they had found a café and were sat inside having a drink of coffee. Jip saw the white car pull into the café, and he watched as the two male occupants came into the cafe. They sat in a corner that was the other side of the room to where Jip was sat.

Jip was convinced they were the police and they were there to make sure he handed himself over to them. It was a good assumption Luci thought.

When they had finished the drinks, Jip went and relieved himself.

Luci organised the back of the LandRover in a way that she could lay down and have a sleep. Jip was paranoid and he jumped at every noise that he heard. Nobody did join him and when he had finished it was back to driving for him. As he drove, Jip was haunted with the thought, that by believing in something, he had become involved in so much controversy. He did not disturb Luci who was in the back asleep. Jip turned into a lane that he knew would lead to the back roads.

It was about 3:30pm and as they trundled on, they came to a little village. Jip noticed that a lot of the posters he had made were advertising the Hill, all over the place! As he left the village and approached a crossroads, Jip was confronted with a Lorry that was straddled across the road, blocking his way! Jip's thoughts immediately told him that this was a trap! But as Jip slowed he noticed an older man who had a jack and a wheel-brace in his hands. He walked to the front of the lorry where Jip saw the tyre was flat! Jip stopped and got out, he asked the driver if he needed help and Jip obliged. Then the white car pulled up behind the LandRover, one of the men stepped out and walked over to where the lorry driver was stood talking to Jip, Jip froze expecting the worse!

"We have a tube of that tyre weld in our boot, it might get you to a garage, oh, there is a compressor that you plug into the cigarette lighter socket, would you like to use that as well?" The suited man from the white car asked.

Jip was jacking the wheel so that it was off of the ground, as the driver acknowledged the offer. The suited man went back to the white car. He retrieved the equipment and he gave it all to Jip! Jip accepted. He watched as the man returned to his car. Jip then found a stone and he jammed it against the rear wheels of the lorry. He unscrewed the valve cover and he screwed on the tyre weld container. After the contents had been put into the tyre. Jip plugged the mini-compressor into the LandRover and sat with the driver while the tyre inflated.

"It might work! How far have you to go?" Jip said.

THE OTHER SIDE OF THE LINE

The driver explained that he was only 5 miles from his base and he started talking men stuff to Jip. The driver then offered Jip a share of the contents of his flask and they both sat waiting for the tyre to inflate.

The white car sat there waiting, other cars had turned up, and they had turned about and gone another route! Jip was anxious and paranoid.

When the tyre was inflated enough, Jip took the lorry off of the jack and he returned the compressor.

Before he reached the car, the suited man came and accepted it off of him. Jip stared him in the eye and the man stared back.

"Thank you" Was all the man said and Jip returned to the driver who thanked him.

Jip helped the driver to manoeuvre the lorry by way of hand signals. He then returned to the LandRover.

Jip began driving again and he watched in his mirror as the white car actually turned off at the next junction. The lorry turned into a yard a little further on and Jip felt relieved. He decided that he would wake Luci, he put his hand over the bulkhead and started to bang it shouting her name. When he did not get a reply! He slowed down to take a look and he was astounded! Luci was not in there! Jip quickly turned the LandRover about and headed back from where he had came from, his heart was pounding and his mind was racing away with completely wild thoughts of kidnap and other things.

Then he turned the last bend and he saw Luci sat on the grass!

She was giggling, and she laughed pointing at him as he arrived.

"I wondered how long it would take you to realise that I was not there!" She laughed.

Luci explained that she had woken up and gone to find somewhere to go to the toilet and when she had returned all the vehicles were gone! After a lot of laughter they were back onto the road.

Everything seemed to be normal as they approached the turning for Valleydale, but as they turned Jip noticed a white car, which was very similar to the one they had encountered earlier.

Jip made himself to feel alert. As they drove passed the white car, Jip felt a weird electrical type feeling run through his head! Luci was oblivious to it and the LandRover turned into the approach to the Hill. "Home beautiful home!" Jip said as the entered the gates.

They were surprised at the stillness of the Hill, there was nobody to be seen, and as he pulled up next to the bus, he saw that the door was open!Jip leapt out of the LandRover and ran with aggression into his bus! He was greeted by two men in a suit, sat on his settee? Jip stopped himself in his tracks; he realised that the two men were the men he had seen earlier in the white car! Before he could speak, the taller of the men stood up and he stood about six feet tall!

"Good evening, we are pleased that you made it safely," The man said.

"What the hell are you doing on my bus?" Jip angrily asked.

The man then explained than they were anti terrorist squad and they wanted to take Jip on a journey!

"How! Where! When! You got a bloody cheek. This is my home!" Jip panicked and he was frightened.

"We are trying a new experiment, it might save people like yourself from going to prison!" The smaller of the two men said.

Jip questioned them of the experiment, he stated that he was not a Guinea pig! The discussion then took a very serious angle?

It was explained that Jip was to be taken by helicopter to a top British intelligence laboratory. He was told that they wanted him to work in a team that would expose bent officials in local Government, the kind who make silly plans that only make them money!

Every thing that was discussed was written on a couple of sheets of paper that the smaller of the two men produced from a case that he had next to him. Jip asked if he could contact his solicitor but he was bereaved at this suggestion. Jip must have been convinced because he signed the paper. He was handed a copy, which he clung to as the men left.Luci had gone to see Judy, as she was scared and thought it would be better if she hid away!

Jip stashed the papers and he went to find her, he knew where she would be. He found her and convinced her that the intruders had left and he told her he would explain everything at a later time. They went back to the bus and Luci went about organising some food. Jip sat and he worked out his explanation to Luci. After they had ate he told her of the plan. She told him that there was a meeting at the café and that must have been why nobody had seen the men arrive! Luci seemed to accept the plan and they made love and slept sound that night.
The next morning, it was John who first saw that the LandRover was back and that meant that Jip and Luci were back!
He went and told the others, they all went to Jip's bus. All Jip saw was Casy's face smiling at him like the sun!
"Hey! Wake up you honeymooners!" Casy laughed.
Once Jip had dressed and drank his first coffee, they all started discussing the last few day's happenings.
Casy had an interesting tale to tell him. He spoke of the police coming and visiting the Hill again!
They said, that if Jip did not return, he was going to be found and remanded in custody! Then the conversation went a diverse way as a point arose over the question of Elaine's loyalty! She had apparently been seen talking with some men who were in suits. The talk went on well into the day and when all had been discussed the bus was peaceful again. The evening was spent with Jip telling Luci that he will miss her, as they had never been apart! He spoke of loyalty and trust. When Jip finally retired, Luci sat up and thought of Pixies and Elves and goblins and the Fairies!The next morning, Jip was awoken early by the noise of his mobile telephone ringing.
When he answered it he said abruptly,
"What is it!"
"Just us checking" Was the reply.
Jip was annoyed; he said words to that fact, down the telephone. The conversation was then over. Jip crept back to his bed making sure he did not disturb Luci.

THE OTHER SIDE OF THE LINE

A few hours past and after a couple of strong coffees, Jip had been joined by Casy. Casy had fed his Horses and rode up to tell Jip some amazing news!

"Suzie is pregnant!" Casy laughed as he spoke.

Jip hugged him and congratulated him,

"Well done my friend" Jip said.

Jip then said that he would tell Luci and he stressed that he was worried that she might become broody! Casy laughed as he saw Luci walk into the room as Jip was saying this!

"Casy! You are going to be a dad! Wow! How will you cope? Nappies, no sleep?" Luci asked laughing.

Casy was deliberate as he told them that he could cope. Jip and Luci sat and stared at the jolly Casy,

Jip was the first to speak, and he said,

"What time is it?"

He was informed that it was creeping towards 11:30am.

Jip thought of a good chance to enjoy themselves, would be a trip to the pub!

"Time to wet the babies head!" Jip said.

"I will go down to fetch Suzie from the bender" Casy said as he shrugged his shoulders and left.

Jip watched him ride off, he was thinking that Casy always seemed to cheer him up. Jip and Luci decided to go and see Suzie. They walked down to her bender. Jip was singing a version of the song 'Congratulations' as they entered the bender. Suzie was overwhelmed and she was really very happy!

Jip left to fetch the LandRover and Casy went and tied his Horse up. Soon they were all loaded into the LandRover.

Jip was driving slowly across the site. Casy noticed a Horse that was being chased by a few of the Horsemen, he asked Jip to stop. They both went. It was Casy who caught the stray animal!

Drink was the mission for the day!

Jip played a game of pool with the father to be!

THE OTHER SIDE OF THE LINE

Luci was discussing names with Suzie. Jip's mobile telephone started to ring in the bar area and he finished his shot before he was handed the telephone from the barman. Luci went over and she grabbed Jip by the arm, she listened as the conversation became discreet and Jip was being niggled. Luci had a feeling that she sensed was fear, her body seemed to go all goose-pimpled and she shuddered as Jip finished the conversation. Casy on the other hand was enjoying a baby's rule the universe moment with Suzie!

Luci was losing her emotions, Jip was thinking. He could tell, she was panicking inside.

Jip went to the table where their drinks were. He slammed his fist on the table in a frustrated way! Luci went over and sat with him, she did not take her eyes off of Jip's lips, and he gave her a quick smile then he spoke,

"Luci, we are going on an adventure."

Casy unwittingly interrupted by saying,

"What is up now Jip?"

Luci thought Casy was being rude and she stormed off to see Suzie, who was trying her hand at playing pool.

"Just a weird invitation" Jip said to Casy.

Jip then went back to drinking with his friend and they had two pints each. Casy then said, he had to sort out the Horses and Suzie said she had things to do, one being a telephone call to her mother! Jip drove them all back to the bus. Jip took Luci and sat her down.

"Tomorrow we will be handing ourselves over to the anti- terrorist squad, They are to investigate the issue of moral judgement on ministers who line their own pockets." Jip was fairly upset as he stated he was scared of the men.He told Luci that they were not the kind of people to mess about with. Ex S.A.S!

"I am willing to give my life to this planet!" He said amorously.

Luci said that she wanted to be with him, wherever he went and Jip agreed with her.

THE OTHER SIDE OF THE LINE

CHAPTER THIRTEEN

Jip was dreaming of a white bird that was carrying him across a Forrest to a castle. When he was over the castle, he peered into the centre courtyard, where he saw a magician standing beside a steaming cauldron that was bubbling.
Then he heard a funny beeping noise and he woke up! He turned off his alarm and he stumbled to put the kettle on. He had to go outside to fetch the water butt, as the kettle needed water. He saw the sun as it came up lighting the sky over the Hill. He sorted out the kettle and he waited until the kettle had boiled and he made the drinks, then he went and he woke the sleeping Luci up. Everything was normal until the mobile telephone sprang into being! Jip had a brief discussion and when he had finished, he turned to Luci and he said,
"We are being collected at 10 o'clock outside of the Library."
"I am quite looking forward to an adventure!" Luci excitedly said.
Jip and Luci had their breakfasts and they had a lot of kisses and a bit of a cuddle. It was then time to leave! They went and said their goodbye's to everyone and Luci ended up in tears as she was thinking that she would miss her friends. Jip left saying,
"We will keep in touch."
Elaine was at the Library as usual; she was reading contentedly from a magazine when she saw a big black limousine pull up outside of the library. She was thinking that it was some famous star looking at her handiwork on the window of the Library. Elaine then found a cloth and she pretended to be cleaning the glass front from inside. She then was distracted by the sound of the LandRover's brakes; they had started to squeal a bit lately! They were a little louder today Jip thought.Jip drove the LandRover so it was behind the limousine. They both jumped out and walked to the limousine. When they had approached the rear of the limousine, the door opened and out stepped two men.

THE OTHER SIDE OF THE LINE

One of the men had a scar that ran the length of his face.
It was his words that were to haunt Luci for a while!
"It's him we want, not you!" The man said.
The two men grabbed Jip by the arms and they pushed him into the rear of the limousine! Soon as they had all clambered into the rear, the limousine drove away!
Luci stood on the pavement totally shell-shocked and in distress!
Jip was thrust back into the seat as the limousine took off! After they had drove out of the village, Jip was offered a glass of claret wine, he accepted this kind offer and he sipped the wine as they travelled, he quite liked the luxury for a few minutes then he shouted,
"Where is Luci, what have you done with her!"
The men calmed him down by telling him that they had left her and he would have the chance to speak with her when they had arrived at their destination. The men then explained that where they were headed, was a secret and nobody was rarely allowed to go there! This alarmed Jip but he smiled and kept composed.After about twenty minutes, Jip went to speak, he tried to say some words but he found his mouth muscles would not work! Slowly he felt all of his body grow numb and he was soon fast asleep! It was a drug-induced sleep!
Back at the library, Elaine was trying to calm the hysterical Luci! She consoled her by telling her it was for the best that she had been left and that Jip was a clever man and nothing would get the better of him! Elaine decided that she would drive Luci back to the bus and get someone to come and get the LandRover, as she felt that Luci was in no state to drive. Poor Elaine was having a lot of trouble calming the crying Luci and she was glad when they reached the Hill.Jip had woken about two hours after he first had fell to sleep. He was still in the back seat of the limousine, but it had stopped and he was on his own! His mind was numb and he still could not lift a limb for about ten minutes, then when he finally came to a near sense.
He stepped out of the limousine, his eyes were blurred in his vision, and he felt groggy. The same two men quickly joined him..

They led him across a car park to a Helicopter!
Jip had never been in one before and he was quite relaxed anyway. He still could only make things out through blurred vision. The men strapped Jip to his designated seat. It was right opposite the open sliding door. Jip focused at a blob, which was a tree, as the helicopter started to rise. He was startled that the tree didn't move! It was not until they were half an hour into the flight that Jip had his sight back.Then he looked at his companions on this experience. He saw that they were wearing a dark black uniform, which had white stripes on the shoulder pads! Jip decided that he must be on a hallucinogenic drug! But the uniform did not change! Jip then found he could speak just and he said,
"This is weird!"
The two men laughed a petty laugh; it was hard enough to hear them anyway because of all the noise that the Helicopter was making. It was about twenty minutes later and they landed. Jip was led to a car and drove from the airstrip to a beautiful quaint cottage. The cottage was a marvel; it seemed to be miles into the country. It was only about two miles from the airstrip in fact.
Jip was again led, to the cottage. He was taken to one of the three bedrooms that were on the top floor.
"This is where you will sleep, dinner will be served at 4 o'clock, you will get a shout, you should try to rest and don't worry you are safe in here!" A very strong looking man pointed to the bed as he spoke.
Jip took the gentleman's advice, as soon as he had left! Jip lay onto the bed, he tried to sleep, but he found his mind was working overtime. He was deliberating his options. He came to the conclusion that he would rather of been where he was, than been in a prison cell. A couple of hours had passed by the time Jip was disturbed by a noise that came from the other side of the door. He went to the door and it opened to his amazement! He felt that he could move freely and he went to investigate, he was especially interested in the position of the bathroom.

When he had accomplished his mission he headed towards the stairs. As he turned the corner he saw a young woman who was busy polishing the brass which laced the stairway. She did not speak and seemed not to really notice Jip as he slipped past. He found himself faced to a wooden door, he suspiciously opened it, and was helped open by one of the two men he had shared company with earlier that day. The men introduced themselves to Jip. The taller one with the scar was Todge; the other one was The Colonel! Jip was then gestured to sit down. He did as he felt he should. He sat down. Jip accepted the invitation to have a cigarette; he expressed a worry about accepting anything to drink,

"After the last time!" He stated.

The Colonel told him that they had to have drugged him for security reasons and that it was necessary!

Then the men discussed the living quarters and Jip started to feel more relaxed and managed a giggle at a comment that Todge made. Jip expressed that he was missing his love, Luci! He was overwhelmed at the response!

"Go and telephone the girl, tell her you are safe!" The Colonel said in a laid back manner.

"Everything is bugged!" Todge said laughing.

Jip decided that he would telephone Luci, he went over to the telephone table that stood in the room. Jip told a few white lies to Luci, he did not tell her of the drug that they had used on him, he instead made out he had a beautiful journey in a Helicopter! She believed him and they talked until the Colonel told them to stop. Jip told Luci that he hoped that he could keep incontact and he would telephone at every opportunity. As he finished his conversation there was a knock on the front door of the house. The room was silent as the colonel distinguished his cigarette and was waiting. A very stern looking man entered the room, he was introduced to Jip as the Duke.

Soon they all sat discussing all that had happened to Jip since the start of the Valleydale affair. He was surprised to learn that he was admired for his commitment and skill of protesting!
This made him feel important and a smile came over his face at last. It was about one hour after the influx of the good feeling vibe that the Colonel walked across to a cabinet and opened a drawer. He brought out a file.
"Here is our assignment chaps!" He said cheerfully.
The Colonel placed the file onto the table and he said.
"Tonight we must rest, tomorrow morning at 6am, we are to fly to the Shetland Islands. Jip is to meet Dr Longthore, who will give you a medical to see if you are fit enough for this assignment, that is all"
The Colonel then left the room. The Duke followed him. Jip thought that it was all very strange! He decided that he would go along with the flow for a while! Jip then asked the Colonel if he could take a walk and grab some fresh air? He was told more or less to not leave the garden, as he would be on camera the whole time. Feeling a little paranoid Jip went out into the Garden. As he explored he found a circle of stones pervading from the earth! They reminded Jip of a set of witches all turned into stone! He considered it a sacred place and it was where he sat deliberating things until he was called for his food. He put on a brave front and he re-entered the cottage. A really delightful banquet of vegetarian cuisine confronted him and he dug well in! The Colonel and Todge ate.
After they told Jip that they would be back for the morning. He was told that he was free to use the amenities as he liked, but never to leave the grounds! Jip was happy as happy could be with this scenario and he sussed the cocktail cabinet out. He poured a glass of white rum and sat beside the telephone, it took him one sip and he telephoned Luci back at the Hill. He did feel a bit strange, as he had never dialled his own telephone number before today. They talked for hours and it was the early morning when they tore themselves away. He went to the bedroom with his head full up with emotions, he fell onto the bed.

Jip managed to get a couple of hours sleep; the Sun had woken him as it gazed powerfully through the open curtains.
Jip heard the birds all twittering away with their melodies. His mind was on how dry his mouth was and not really on his situation and he staggered down the stairs. He again saw the young woman cleaning, this time she spoke.
"Breakfast is served in the main room," She said.
Jip thanked her and he entered the main room through the wooden door. His first sight was of the Colonel who was eating a meat sausage!
"You do understand, I am a vegetarian?" Jip spoke with a croak.
The Colonel told him that they all were aware he was! To Jip, he looked a little hung over.
Jip went to the coffee percolator that was in the room; he offered everyone a cup before he poured his own. Then as he sat and took his first sip, the young woman brought in the breakfast. The Breakfast was another fabulous vegetarian one and Jip ate heartily.
The breakfast was over very soon for Jip and the conversation had started flowing. They talked of conservation, the wild life creatures seemed very dominant.
"We have to be leaving now,"
Todge said as he stood up and gestured Jip to the door.
Jip followed the Colonel and before he had realised, they were in another limousine and they drove away from the cottage. Jip did not have any time to gaze out of the window as the Colonel was holding his attention by pointing at pieces of paper; he explained the day's action to him.
"First we will visit the doctor, then we will join the ship H.M.S. Alacticity. It will take us to the Shetland isles, where the secret base that stores the chemicals is. Look, don't question me! I feel you are intelligent enough to understand! Everything will become apparent as the day goes on."
Todge then interrupted,

THE OTHER SIDE OF THE LINE

"Here we are, You will enjoy this Jip!"
"I have a slight weary mind this morning" Jip Stated.
"None of that! You're a man not a mouse are you not?" The Colonel remarked and that grin was back on his face.
Jip cringed and he gazed out of the window for the first time, he was busy looking as the Limousine drove down a lane to a derelict piece of Land, which had a Chinook Helicopter sat there! Both of its rotor-blades were turning!
The Colonel introduced the Helicopter as American made. Jip had a panic attack inside of him, he managed to control it just as the limousine stopped, he was ushered out. The colonel led him at a trot and soon they were aboard the Helicopter!
Jip was shown how to strap himself in, then as he was finishing his stomach felt as if it had fallen out of his body! It was the lift of the take off! Todge undid his own belt and slide the side door open, Jip watched as he saw greenery for miles and miles, it was beautiful. The Landscape was magnificent. Jip was amazed! He started to enjoy the experience! Todge was watching Jip and he started to shout over the noise pointing out the Landmarks.
Jip could just about make out a couple of the words, he smiled and nodded his head when he thought necessary! To Jip it was becoming like riding a roller coaster! After they had been flying for about half an hour, Jip saw the water appear it did not seem to be very far away, the Helicopter was flying low across the water! Jip felt a twitter in his stomach and he felt for the men who had lost their lives on the oilrigs. The nerves disappeared when he spotted a fishing boat and it reminded him of Cornwall. It was not very long and they were back over land. The landscape was one of trees and a few patches of barren land. Todge sat down and he strapped himself in and Jip noticed the Helicopter start to descend amongst the trees!Jip closed his eyes as the Helicopter gently came to a thud! His legs were like jelly and he waited for instruction.Todge unclipped his belt and undid Jip's, he ushered them out, and again at a trot they ran to an Army LandRover.

Jip nearly fell once and it was all that he could do was to stay on his feet! Jip sat in the back watching as the vehicle moved away.

He saw a couple of deer's, then a buzzard. A magpie was sitting on a gate as they passed. This hampered Jip's mood, he considered a single Magpie as a sign!

For bad luck!

He was relieved when as they were nearly out of view, another magpie gracefully sailed next to the other. Jip felt a big wave of relief run through his body!

Nobody spoke as they trundled along a dirt track that was definitely British! Jip was becoming paranoid, as they seemed to be going for miles into the middle of nowhere! The Weather was drizzle that turned into a heavy shower and the rest of the journey was spent dodging the drips of water that came from the tarpaulin cover. The LandRover then came to a stop and Jip was ushered out, he stood in the rain looking at Todge. The Colonel talked on the radio in the cab. Jip decided that it was time he spoke, he gathered up as much dignity that he could positively muster.

"Where might the doctor be?" He said slowly becoming wet as the weather was back to it's casual dribble of misty rain.

Todge held him by the shoulder and he pointed across to a bank of land. He led Jip's arm to point at the hilly terrain.

Jip was astonished as his eyes became fixed on a metal clad door that seemed to be moulded into the landscape!

As this was happening, the Colonel stepped out of the LandRover, he led them over to the door.

Jip turned as he saw the LandRover turn and leave.

The ground was rough as he gazed at it, waiting for the door to open. The Colonel had banged the door twice in an orderly way.

Then he banged it three times in quick succession.

The door swung open and Jip noticed that the hinges were well oiled! They all entered; the Colonel led with Jip sandwiched in the middle.

Jip saw that they were in a small room that had two cameras in it, they were facing another door and waiting for it to open. Jip felt uneasy and he started to fidget with his jacket.

It seemed to take an eternity to Jip, the door then slid open, and they entered a lift! He was distracted, they had to shuffle around so that they all could fit, into the lift. Then the door closed, they were descending, and it seemed to Jip to go down for miles! It was the longest lift he had ever been in! The lift finally stopped and the door was once again opened, they all stepped out and were greeted by what Jip considered to be a Troll. That was his first impression anyway! The man was wearing spectacles and his hair stood on end! There were a lot of handshakes and a few formalities all strangely revealed. Jip was invited to go into another room with the man; he was quite relaxed as he went in. He saw a dentist type chair and he sat into it. The man, who was the doctor. Started to place electrodes onto his chest. Jip undressed his top half-first. The doctor said.

"This one will check your lungs and this one your heart" As he placed the electrodes on to Jip's body.

Jip watched as the doctor turned a machine on and a wavy line appeared. Jip recognised the machine to be a monitor.

Then the doctor started to place the electrodes onto his neck and Jip was frightened when he placed them on to his temples!

"No way! Not today mate!" Jip said in a subtle way.

"Oh come on! It will tell me about your blood pressure!"The doctor said pushing one of the electrodes to Jip's left temple!

Jip could not stop himself, he flew up from the chair, and he freaked out ripping the electrodes from his body as he did. As he fumbled untying him he felt a surge of bodies grab him; he felt a sharp pain in his thigh!It was as if magic had been performed!

Jip lost all of his emotion and a wave of peace flowed through his body. His hearing became deranged and his vision became tunnelled. None of the changes seem to effect him as he was enjoying the feeling.

The doctor was not a happy man and he told Todge that they would go to plan B, what ever that was! Jip did not hear anything as his hearing was picking up the high pitched noise of the monitor machine.

It did not again seem to bother him at all!The doctor went to a cupboard and he produced a piece of amethyst and placed in on the side where he knew Jip would see it.

Jip was trying to focus on the room and it was about five minutes later that his tunnel vision spotted the crystal. His mind told him that it was Merlin's crystal and that he was powerful! He tried to speak; his mouth did not want to move a muscle, so he gave up. Todge came in and he walked straight up to Jip, Jip did not see him, as the crystal was so beautiful. Todge was taking the Mickey when he said,

"We are magicians, we need your help to find the key master!"

Jip heard this and he believed the crystal was talking with him!

Todge then casually picked up the crystal and holding it so Jip could focus on it he started to move out of the room. Jip followed the crystal, he found that it was easy to walk, he was struggling with his vision and speech. He saw what he thought were the planets floating in front of him! They were in fact the backs of Todge and the Colonels heads! Todge led Jip for ages, in through another sliding door, Jip convinced himself that they were entering a space ship! It was a room that had plush white leather furniture, the walls were a sea of machinery, and there were screens and flashing lights! In the middle of the room was a casual coffee table. On the table was piping hot coffee! Jip sat down with Todge, as he knew the crystal was in Todge's pocket. A cup was placed into his hands. As he raised the cup to his mouth, Jip heard a strange kind of rushing noise and a bright red dot appeared in the centre of the table!

"Jip! We have drugged you and we need you to tell us when your vision is back to normal!" He heard.

With that, Jip felt another pain, this time it was in his arm! His vision seemed to broaden out and Jip felt extremely tired, he fell to sleep!

THE OTHER SIDE OF THE LINE

Todge saw this and he just about grabbed the hot coffee from Jip's hand before it dropped. Smiling he turned to the Colonel and said.
"Let's go to the canteen, we can lock him here and he will sleep at least an hour, we can put it in the report!"
Jip was left slouched on the sofa sleeping soundly.
Jip was woken after he felt a sharp pain in his neck! He suddenly could hear again!
"Jip can you see me yet?" Todge asked him.
All Jip saw was darkness, gradually his sight did come back and a related Jip declared.
"Yes! I can see you!"
Todge then asked him what colour shirt that he was wearing. Jip looked him up and down, he saw that he had army boots with army trousers and an army shirt, which was green. He told him the colour Todge said.
"We have a lot to do if we are going to sort out this planet!"
Jip relaxed, as he really had no idea of what was going on, his mind was blank and he felt dazed. It was about ten minutes later that Jip felt well enough to stand up. He discovered that all he could concentrate on was his present situation, which was standing up! Jip did not notice the Colonel when he entered.
"Are you ok Jip?" The Colonel politely asked.
Jip turned and saw the Colonel and acknowledged that he was fine.
"Good, it is time to continue with our tasks.
We are going to locate the chemicals.
Then try and find a way to dispel them without upsetting anyone!" The Colonel was serious.
Jip acknowledged the Colonels words with the nod of his head; he then followed the Colonel out of the door and to the lift.
Jip could not decipher whether they were going vertical or down! When the lift stopped, he realised that they were in a giant underground tunnel. Wall-mounted lights lit up and it smelt of Diesel!

He followed as the Colonel led him over to a yellow coloured electric vehicle. Jip saw it was a half jeep half milk float when they became closer. They all leapt on board. They trundled; Jip could see men's faces! They were sentries that were posted on each hundred-yard marker. Jip felt oblivious to any danger and he felt quite special.

The jeep suddenly came to a jerky halt. Jip saw that they had stopped at the entrance of a cave. When he stepped off the vehicle he could hear the slapping of water. It all became clearer as the Colonel guided them along a thin path with high sidewalls. It revealed a jetty where a ship was tied.

Next to the ship was a crane, which was loading crates onto the ship. "Food for our journey" Todge said to Jip who nodded.

They all then briskly walked to the gangplank and were piped on board. Jip hit his head as they entered a steel door; it did not seem to bother him as he clambered down some highly polished wooden stairs. He was taken to a lounge area and Jip was impressed at the comfort. He sat down and a woman in a Royal Navy uniform came over and handed him a menu! Jip, Todge and the Colonel all ordered food. The wren wrote it all down and said it would take about twenty minutes. Todge followed her and he fetched a decanter. The decanter was full of orange juice, Jip watched him and the Colonel drink from it before he did!

Lunch arrived and as they ate, Jip felt the ship gently start to move. He still was feeling safe and any doubt he did have was lost when the Colonel said.

"We will go to the bridge and meet the captain after lunch!"

When they had all finished eating and drinking, the Colonel led them down a passageway. Jip saw a room with a lot of computers in it as they walked. Then they came to some more highly polished stairs and they walked up onto the bridge. Jip looked around and his attention was on the open sea that he could see out of the front glass.

Todge asked Jip if he would like to steer the ship, he declined, as he did not feel he could. After gazing for a while he was introduced to the Captain and they shook hands, everything was formal and very polite! Soon the party left the bridge and they stepped out onto the deck, the Colonel stressed that he was cold but Jip felt warm. He was enjoying watching the open sea and he liked the way the ship was gliding along in it.

They were however soon into another room; Jip saw a television screen that was showing a video. It was paused and Todge picked up the remote control and he pressed the play button.

Jip could not believe his eyes, on the screen appeared pictures of him and Luci! It showed all of Jip's friends as well! The picture showed all of the protests that Jip had been included in; the last picture was of Stonehenge about ten years previously, which was before the fence had ruined the sight! Jip was there, he was surprised at how young he looked.

"We have the footage of every protest that has ever gone on!" The Colonel said staring at Jip.

"I have tried for years to make the public to become aware of the environmental struggle that we have to face." Jip replied having being jolted by the tape.

"We can understand your frustrations Jip, we can agree with most but!" The Colonel paused as he spoke.

The Colonel went to a case that was in the room and he brought out a file.

"All of the Governments! In the world, have came to the same conclusion over the fate of planet Earth! It is now known that the Earth is in fact off of its axis! It is only a few degrees off, we think it has been caused by the nuclear bombs that were tested,on the surface of the planet! Anyway it is concluded that every government has been part of the mistake. The problems that face us are that the earth will be closer to the sun and the intense heat would cause all of the chemicals in our world to become deadly hot and this would cause a chemical reaction which would be highly dangerous!

So my boy, this is what we need you for! We have to find a solution, either by putting the planet back onto its axis or by dispelling the chemicals so that they are safe. Time on the other hand is not really on our side, we have calculated that in twenty years time the earth will become human-less!" The Colonel frightened Jip when he again showed his evil grin.
Jip asked if the chemicals could form defences layers and actually cool the planet.
Todge gave him a quick shake of the head
"There is no way of knowing what we can successfully achieve, so Jip we want your mind to help us find this solution, we wont need you to tell us any details of the chemicals but if you have a view then please tell us!" The Colonel stopped talking and he sipped a glass of water.
It was deadly quiet and Jip was as quiet as the next man was.

CHAPTER FOURTEEN

It was just about daylight in Valleydale; Luci was just waking up still clutching a picture of Jip in her hands,
"Please phone today you rat!" She said to herself.
Luci made herself a hot drink, as she drank she looked down the valley to the village through the bus window. She saw the postman and his van and she wondered if Jip had written to her?
Suzie was kind of looking after her, as well as coping with her pregnancy, so Luci was not surprised when Suzie entered the bus. After they had greeted each other with the good morning sentence, Luci told her that she wanted to go to the studio under the library to see if Jip had wrote to her. Suzie was pleased, as Luci was sounding a little more positive today! Then to Suzie's great joy Luci explained that she had arranged to have lunch with Elaine and Alex. This meant that Suzie could go to the village with Casy without having to tow Luci along!Casy was busy feeding his Horses when he saw John who had risen from his dreamland. John asked if Casy wanted any breakfast and he accepted. John then started to collect the wood for a fire to heat the food.
Luci became excited when the mobile telephone rang, but it was only Elaine confirming the lunch date.
Luci was sad as she missed Jip with all of her heart. After she had checked the library basement for post, after finding no letter from Jip, she walked up to the top of the Library where Elaine was really busy.
"The rat has still not wrote to me!" Luci said as she greeted Elaine.
"Luci, I will be about ten minutes, then we shall see what Alex has to say ok?" Elaine replied.
After fumbling through books for ten minutes, Elaine was finally ready and she grabbed her coat and gave Luci a shout.
Luci was reading a book on Geography.
"Come on! Let's have a good wholesome lunch!"
Elaine said as she locked the Libraries doors.

Elaine led Luci to the Valleydale arms and when they entered the pub, Alex was sat next to the window. Luci sat with him as Elaine went to the bar and she ordered some drinks.

"I have some great news for you!" Alex said as she joined him.

Luci pleaded with him to let her out of her misery, and Alex obliged after a prompt from Elaine who had fetched the drinks.

"You are to go and stay with Jip! You will help him on his secret project!" Alex told her.

He said that she was to be ready in two days time and that he would pick her up at the bus, nine o'clock sharp in the morning!

Luci was thrilled and she bought a round of drinks to celebrate, they all then drank a toast to Jip and Luci! They ordered their lunches and after they had eaten it, Elaine said that she had the afternoon off.

She asked Luci if she would like to join her? A drive in the country was her plan.

Elaine drove with Luci to the Breacon Beacons, where they walked up another hill; they could just make Valleydale out from the top ridge.

"Two days" Was all anyone could hear from Luci when she returned to the bus?

Suzie, Casy, Judy, and Luci lit a fire and they all sat around it looking at the stars.

The next morning, Luci was out quite early. She had seen Casy and asked if she could ride one of his Horses, he had agreed and said he would lend her Star. Star was an older Horse who was used to being ridden.Luci had done her rounds and she had picked up the Horse, she rode all about the Hill speaking to everyone she saw! Most actually thought that she was nearly back to her old self again. The day passed peacefully and Judy cooked tea for Luci, Suzie, Casy, John, and herself, she did this on the bus and they all ate a delicious meal. After the food they all drank Casy's homemade wine and sat talking, getting drunk until the early hours of the morning. When Luci finally went to bed she laid for hours dreaming of Jip.

She was sure she had seen his face in front of her, he told her that he was safe and well. It was after this, that she did fall sound asleep!

The morning came and Luci was nowhere to be seen when Alex came to meet her, he knocked hard on the bus door, it took Luci about two minutes to answer his call.

"Are you ready? The plane leaves in an hour and it will take us forty minutes to get to the airport!"

Alex said as he greeted the hungover Luci.

"You never said anything about an aeroplane?" Luci stammered.

Luci ran indoors and she grabbed the holdall that she had packed about a week before and she locked the bus door as she left. She jumped into Alex's car and he drove her to the airport. When they had entered the airport terminal Alex gave her the ticket and said,

"You will be met at the other end so just enjoy your flight!"

Luci read her ticket and it said that she was leaving from terminal three, Alex showed her the way and he stayed to wave her off as she boarded the plane. She was lucky that she had been allocated a window seat and it was also in the smoking area! She lit a cigarette and sat back, her poor tummy was turning with the excitement of it all.

The aeroplane took off safely and they flew for an hour.

Once she had landed and disembarked, she stood in the lounge area waiting for someone to pick her up as Alex had said.

"Could Luci on flight 475 please attend desk three?" The tannoy remarked.Luci followed her instructions and a woman who was very smartly dressed met her,

"Luci? Good. Your carriage awaits" The woman said pointing her finger to the main entrance.

THE OTHER SIDE OF THE LINE

CHAPTER FIFTEEN

Back at the cottage. Jip was excited of the plan to have Luci to join him. He had visited the chemical plant and had organised to return, as the man who was to have shown him the chemicals, was unavailable because of some crisis. Jip had become much more at ease, the last day was his best, he had been told of Luci Joining him, he tried to phone her but he was at sea until late that evening, he was dog tired when he returned.Jip felt something that he had almost forgotten about. It was Love! His heart pounded and his stomach fluttered! It was nearly the time that she was due to land! Jip had been told that the journey from the airport was only about twenty minutes. The colonel and Todge was rib tickling him over Luci joining him!

It was the Colonel who took a message on his radio; it was that the car that was carrying Luci had arrived. It was parked in front of the cottage. Jip was told and he ran out to greet her. It was as if it were magic! They were again back in each other's arms.

The colonel and Todge were both married and they made themselves scarce after telling Jip that the rules still applied. That was the cottage and its garden were the only place they could go!

"This cottage is beautiful," Luci said as the Colonel and Todge left them alone.

Jip remarked on how the two of them could cause a security scare. He moaned on at Luci about the cameras and he knew well that the telephone was bugged. He explained in a funny way that only Luci would understand, about how he thought that there were microphones in the house! She played along with that and she said,

"Where is the kitchen? I'm hungry after that flight!"

They then cooked together and drank the beer that was in the fridge and Lovemaking was the subject of the night.

The next morning was strange as Jip had Luci to wake up too. Jip had been to the bathroom when the telephone had rang down the stairs. He answered it, and was told that he had twenty-four hours of peace!

THE OTHER SIDE OF THE LINE

Todge told him that he was having a break from him and the Colonel was too! It was explained that a parcel would be delivered, and that Jip must sign for it. He said he would.

Breakfast was a hearty affair as Luci unleashed her talents in the very modern kitchen. They had quite a laugh trying to work the electric tin opener! Jip though, had a feeling deep in his stomach; it was something he was not sure of!

Once the breakfast was eaten, the package arrived, it was from the back door of the cottage, and as Jip opened the back door, he was amazed to be confronted by a hooded soldier who did not speak but gave him the envelope. He made a gesture for Jip to sign, he did, and the soldier was gone! Jip and Luci were sat in the big room and they opened the envelope as it was addressed to them both. The document was a very official looking on and it accompanied a file. The letter was an easy explanation, in the basement of the cottage there was a computer, and in it was the disk that was concerned with the equation. Jip wanted out! It was too heavy for him he thought. Luci loved anything electrical and she pressed Jip to show her the room. Jip had to discover its entrance, himself! They found it under the stairs and there was a light at the top, which when they switched it on, the whole of the room became alive. The room was quite a nice affair, the computer was the main feature, and Luci was soon on it following the instructions that she received via the screen. She had to log on and she managed to do it successfully! Then she needed a code, this proved harder as Jip had gone upstairs for something.

He had taken the file with him! So once she had hunted him down and retrieved the file she went back to the computer. As soon as she had pressed the Enter key, the screen showed a face, which spoke to her! "Chemical warfare, a synopsis of biographical information."

Jip heard the voice as it was fairly loud and he joined Luci, the woman's face did seem familiar after a while and they listened intently to it. Jip heard of how Galoc Four was a chemical that had been in storage since 1952 and of how it had become unstable!

The Chemical still had no neutralisation agent.
The computer image then stated that the 'module' had finished.
Luci went and made some drinks and when she rejoined Jip he was messing with the computers mouse. He really did not have any idea of how to use it!
"Luci that is why they need us both!" Jip shouted starting to return to his old self.
Luci just told him that the chemical should be placed in another container and zapped into space!
As she finished her speech a voice appeared from behind them. They both turned startled! They saw an older man who was wearing a white coat!
"I am the Professor, I have been given the task of helping you realise the implications of any ideas that you have." The professor said.
Jip remarked on how it all felt like going back to school to him!
"Galoc Four?" Jip said as he sat down.
The Professor said that he wanted to aquaint himself with him formally first, he sat talking formal things.
Luci offered tea and she went and made some.
The professor told Jip of the great importance this project was.
"Galoc Four is a composition mainly composed of Nicro-Mercury Z-4, which in lay mans terms mean, it's a gas that if mixed with Oxygen then it would react! This chemical reaction would render any human, animal or plant dead in about thirty seconds!It is stored in Scotland under a Hill and is so volatile that any movement or change in the temperature would cause it to react!" The professor was deadly serious as he spoke.
Luci entered the room with the drinks and she sat and she joined them,
"We will have to find a way to make this gas harmless, or we can dispel it, to where it would not harm many things." The professor continued talking.
"What we need is a viable solution to moving the case.

Take in the mind that the canister is sixteen inches square? The temperature must not go above fifteen Fahrenheit!"

The professor stopped and sipped his tea. Jip was intrigued, he could not believe that he was being told about the gas and that he could make a difference in the way it was dispelled! Jip had a couple of poignant questions for the professor,

"How was the chemical taken to Scotland in the first place?" He asked.

The professor thought for a moment. He told Jip that the chemical was actually made in Scotland by some foreign terrorists. He stated that they had not been from any part of the British Isles.

Jip took it all in! He was flabbergasted that the Government had not the technology to sort this task!

He cockily said,

"Why don't you isolate the box into a big room, fill the room with ice and freeze it until it becomes a solid and then decompose it in some way?"

The professor laughed at him and told him that the problem had been with them for many years and that he just wanted Jip to realise the difficulties they had, trying to remedy it. Jip lit a cigarette and he was slowly getting the picture!

"Surely there must be a chemical that would mix with the Mercury and dilute the potency?" Jip questioned.

He was told that Mercury was a very volatile chemical that was very difficult to transfuse into another form than it's original! Jip then realised that he was out of his depth, he was not a scientist, and he did not want to become one! He had one thing clear in his head; Galoc Four was to be the gas, which they were to expel from the Hill! The Professor saw this change in Jip's mental state and he turned military styled around and he left the building. Jip followed him up the stairs and he watched as the professor open the door of his jaguar motor car and drive away. Luci offered to make some lunch.

Jip agreed it would be a fantastic idea.

Jip went and sat in the kitchen with Luci and during lunch he stated, that he did not know why they had been brought to the cottage and Luci said,
"At least we are not in prison!"
Jip was still thinking of a way to dispel Galoc Four and he came up with a plan to use sand and sponges that would be soaked in an alkaline liquid. Luci laughed and she was sure it was all out of her depth.
After lunch the pair relaxed in the living room and mid-way throughout he afternoon the Colonel and Todge arrived.
The Colonel was dressed in a combat uniform and he had a deadly serious look on his face when he entered and said,
"Here is a floppy disc for the computer, on it is the Governments guide to how a chemical should be treated!"
The Colonel placed the disc onto the table, this gave Luci a Que., and she vacated to the kitchen and returned with hot drinks for them all.
The colonel took a sip and he started to explain of the idea of section 48.
"Valleydale was chosen because of its geographical position, it was worked out that if the chemical was released there, it would travel in the air to the North or South poles. This would be dependant on the weather conditions and that it was planned to monitor the movement of the gas!"
Jip was interested, but he did not seem satisfied that the chemical was to be allowed to freely pollute the atmosphere in a hope that it would be sucked up the hole in the ozone layer! Jip was astounded when Todge butted in and said,
"In Parliament on Wednesday, there is to be a meeting, it will decide the fate once and for all!"
He explained that the decision could go to reinstating section 48 or totally abandoning it.
Jip was told that himself and Luci were to attend to view their opinions to the ministers. The Colonel stepped in and said,

"Don't debate this with us, you will have your chance on Wednesday!"

The Colonel then left, Todge said that they would be back in the morning.

Jip realised a lot of truths about section 48 and he was scared! His stomach was rioting and his heart again started pounding. His mind started to panic and he ran to the back door where he was physically sick down the drain! Luci made him a drink, but Jip went to the sink and he drank straight from the tap. He then went out to the garden and he sat by the riverside starring at the trickling water. He noted a Dragonfly, which was sitting on a precariously angled stone that was emerging from out of the water. Jip washed his face with the cold spring water. He was thinking that the water would cleanse him, he did not consider he had been cleansed enough, so he stepped into the small stream, he laid flat onto his back into the water!

His body was totally immersed; he was enjoying the trickle of water, which made a passage around his face. He stayed in the position for at least ten minutes.

Luci decided that she would go and find him as she was feeling a little scared on her own, she too, ended up at the stream and she took her shoes and socks off and started to paddle her feet in a spiral fashion as they dangled into the water. She looked at the stars.

Jip watched her intently and he was sure that she had not noticed him! He leapt up out of the water and he stated,

"What a beautiful evening!"

Luci leapt to her feet startled, and they laughed together. When they had finished skylarking about, Jip stared into her eyes and she saw the frightened child look. He told her he needed time to think and she said she was tired. She went to bed, while Jip took the floppy disc down to the basement where he spent the evening reading the pages that were on the disc. When he had finished he closed the computer down and joined Luci who was sound asleep,

"We have got to leave!" He said as he climbed into the bed.

CHAPTER SIXTEEN

After deliberating for a couple of days, Jip and Luci were ready for the journey that would take them to meet the ministers, who were involved in the Valleydale affairs? A car arrived early and they were taken at speed to London, which meant they had a twenty-minute helicopter ride!

By the time they had arrived in London, they had been travelling for three hours. They were taken to number 2 Downing Street!

When they had entered, Jip and Luci were directed to stand in a room that had a giant table. There they stood gazing at the portraits that were hung on the walls around them. Jip saw one of King George and a smaller one of King Arthur the Legend. Luci saw the second picture

Arthur: King of legend

and she smiled at Jip. The room was empty but for the table and around ten chairs, Jip started to look around to find an ashtray! He found one, up on a shelf and he sat and lit a cigarette. Luci sat next to him, she was starting to get annoyed with the whole affair! They had not been in the room for very long when Todge appeared, he beckoned them to follow him. Jip put his cigarette out and he followed Todge to another big wooden door, as they entered, Todge told them to take deep breaths!

Jip and Luci were suddenly in a room, which was larger than the previous, and there were twelve highly smartly dressed people.

Every one of them looked deadly serious! Jip led Luci to their allotted seats and they sat near to the table. There was a lot of official jargon, as the meeting was declared open!

Two hours it took, until Jip heard his name mentioned!

He was asked to stand and give his full name and his address! Jip told them that he lived at the Hill in Valleydale! They all took this in, each wrote on a piece of paper.

It was then time to leave as the meeting was adjourned until the morning, Jip was thinking that it was a waste of working people's taxes!

Jip and Luci were driven to a house in Bond Street, it was a very large house and when they were shown to where they had to stay, it was a three bedroom flat that was inter-linked to some rooms on the ground floor. But the flat was on the first floor and Jip and Luci had to walk up a flight of stairs to get there. Feeling tired Jip and Luci both went to the bedroom and they fell deep asleep.

It was about four o'clock in the morning! Jip and Luci had been awoken! From down the stairs came a piercing scream! It had woke Jip and Luci immediately! Jip went to the toilet and when he was in the bathroom he heard a lot of shouting, he could not make out what it was all about! He decided to investigate, but as he reached the top of the staircase, he heard two loud bangs and he saw two men clad in black with hoods run out of the front door, Jip was too scared as he had recognised the sounds as gunshots! Jip froze at the top of the stairs; he thought to himself of how one of the two men he saw running away had an object that looked like a pistol in his hands! Getting his courage together, Jip went down the stairs and he started to search the rooms, he was not sure where the shots had been fired! He tried two rooms before he found out! He entered and saw a bed with two men sat on it with gunshot wounds to their heads! Well that was what it looked to Jip, he did not stay around and he quickly closed the door behind him. He melted to the floor and feeling sick he belched as he heard the sound of police sirens growing louder by the second! The hallway where he was lit up in twenty second intervals by a bright blue light! Luci had dressed and saw the state of Jip.

She was the one who jogged him to see sense.

She pulled him up and she said,

THE OTHER SIDE OF THE LINE

"Jip! Let's get the hell out of here!"
Jip did reel to his senses and he led Luci to the back of the house, they found themselves in the kitchen, just as the police rushed the front door! On the side, Luci found a set of keys, they had stickers on a plastic fob, the stickers indicated that one was for the garage. The other for a B M W motor car. Jip finally found the back way out of the house, the pair ran towards the back yard gate which they found was easy to open, Jip ran into the street and he saw that at the farthest end was a set of garages! He ran and tried the key into every lock, which was until he found the lock that accepted the key. He opened the up an over door and inside he found a sparkling B M W motor car! He tried the remote thatwas a button on the keypad and the indicators of the car flashed to say it was ready! Jip went around to the passenger side and he was just opening it as Luci joined him, she slid into the passenger's seat. Jip started the engine after fumbling around with the key trying to find the ignition switch. The engine roared into action and Jip reversed out into the yard and at speed he made his getaway! On the biggest road, which he had taken, they passed three police cars that were zooming with all of their lights flashing in the opposite direction, to where Jip was heading. It did not take them long to find the motorway and they were soon driving at speed along it. There they were, travelling in a brand new car at 100 miles an hour in the fast lane of the motorway! Luci had just become accustomed to the speed and she started to investigate the interior of the car.

On the rear seat she found two sports bags. After she carefully grabbed them and placed them on her lap, she opened them to view the contents! She was astonished to find a tent and a camp kitchen with food in one of the bags, in the other was two sets of waterproof clothing, the ones that you would wear on a boat?

Luci told Jip of her find and after he had calmed down and steadied his driving. He too looked about the car to see if he could see anything that they might need!

Looking in the door compartment he found a brown envelope that was thick to hold. He placed it on Luci's lap and she said that they would open it when they stop, this was because she considered the interior of the car to be too dark.

Jip told her to put the interior light on, but Luci stressed she needed to go to the toilet. Jip turned the car off of the motorway and he started to head along a B road, he saw a Forrest area and he pulled the car into it. Stopping the car, he grabbed the envelope as Luci jumped out and she attended to her business. Jip ripped the envelope open and as he did he saw a lot of twenty pound notes! Which were wrapped in a piece of paper. Jip found it a bit too strange and he thought for a while before he read the note. The note read,

To the seeker,

      THE KEY HAS BEEN LOST! You must find the professor before it is too late!

When or if you succeed, you should tell him these words,

The glow of the crystal will heal the wounds; a blow on the crystal will clear all wrongs! So mote it be!

You will find the answers in a book that is amongst the provisions that have been allocated to you.

      THE PROFESSOR

Jip pondered on the meaning and he visualised the purple crystal that he had encountered. He could not place where that had been as so much had gone on the last week or so! He could not stop seeing the two men who were obviously dead he thought.

He kept visualising the blood that was seeping slowly out of their heads! Luci then returned and she did not see what he had seen and she was rather bubbly.

"It is a game and we have no choice but to play it!" Jip said to her.

Jip then told her of what he called the murder of a couple of gay people. Luci asked him of how sure he was that the men were dead? Jip stated what he had saw and Luci reminded him that it was fairly dark.

She tried to tell him that the light might have been playing tricks on him! Jip dismissed her and he said,

"No matter what I saw! We are not going to be in London for the meeting today are we? Because we have disappeared, they are going to want to now why and how?" Jip felt his mouth go dry.

Luci read the note and she said she was excited because they had a new car and a wad of money! Jip smiled and he decided to find the book, as he was interested to find out about the Professor. Luci said why did they not go to the Hill and get the tickets and find a way of getting to Egypt! Jip had heard enough and he stormed out of the car and he went to open the boot! Luci followed him and she hugged him and apologised for not being sensitive to him. Jip was in turmoil!

"Luci we have been implicated in a murder! For heavens sake will you not understand?" Jip was looking straight into Luci's face as he spoke.

"We did not do it! You know that and so do I!" Luci said.

Jip sat down leaning against the rear bumper, he waited for Luci to join him.

"Luci, the police are obviously setting us up! They have always been slimy against any form of protests, think of the miners and the tales some of them could tell you, and of the original peace convoy and the Beanfield! If we don't go through with this stupid game then we will end up in prison!" Jip was panicking as he spoke.

Luci opened the boot and she saw a plain covered book sat innocently alone. She picked it out and again sat with Jip. They both read the first page. It was an advertisement for a posh restaurant in Edinburgh. At the bottom of the page it read Proprietor Professor Campbell.

"That's it Scotland!" Luci shouted!

Jip saw what was happening and he new he had to follow the plan, he asked Luci if she had found a map?

She had and produced it, he spread the map out over the closed boot lid. On the map Jip pencilled a line to Scotland, he had to start at Birmingham as he had no idea of their true position.

He was sure he had taken the south motorway and he thought that he might be in the New Forrest, which is in Hampshire! Luci had the plan as she said she was hungry and the car would need fuel. The pair felt closer and after a giant hug they climbed back into the car. It took them a quarter of a tank of fuel and a couple of argument's before they found a garage and an answer to all of the questions that they had faced. They were now in Portsmouth and Jip was tempted to try and get on the ferry! Luci talked him into driving to Scotland, she stressed that she had never visited the mainland and she would like too! Jip felt obliged and he marked the map again, he decided that it would be best to travel the B roads and that was what they did. Jip filled the car with petrol and they headed off.

Luci slept for most of the journey and Jip's eyes were a bloodstained mess as they arrived into Edinburgh!

"I need coffee and food!" Jip stammered as he spoke.

"Drive into there!" Luci said waking up and spotting a long stay car park.

Jip did as she instructed and soon they were walking with the book in Jip's hand. Jip was studying the advert and after walking around for twenty minutes they found the restaurant. Jip was surprised that the restaurant was actually open for business, it was early in the morning! The restaurant was very elaborate. Jip felt out of place and he was extremely tired and unshaven.

He decided that they would sit in a dark corner and he chose the one that was nearest to the kitchen area. They ordered a giant meal each. Jip drank two cups of coffee as soon as they arrived.

The meals did not take long and after they had been eaten, Luci said to Jip,

"Why did you kill those two men!"

Jip was flabbergasted and he told her straight that he did not shoot them! What would have been his motive! He complained. Luci then explained that if he reacted the same way, when asked by the police, they would have to believe him!

Jip just could not believe what Luci was speaking of, so he ordered more coffee and he used the toilet. While he was away Luci was handed the bill, with it was another note. She placed the paper on the table and she looked about but the place seemed to be bare of people! She did not see who ever had brought the bill as she was busy eating her sweet and she ignored everyone around her as she enjoyed it! Jip returned and Luci gave him the note, the bill was extravagant in itself, but Jip was more in to reading the note, he asked Luci to settle the bill and she took the envelope that contained the money to the counter.
To Jip and Luci,

          I am pleased to see that you have come this far! If you want to clear your names of
murder! You will have to accept this task! The task is to find a boat and to do this you must find Sam.
You will travel by car and you will drive along the M6 to Glasgow and then the A62 and you will find Sam.

          Good luck,   THE PROFESSOR.

Jip read the note. He was now so sure that it was the police who had set them up, it was so they could not attend the meeting over section 48! Jip declared this to Luci; she took it in and started to realise the same. They left the restaurant in a hurry and they cleverly went to a mobile phone shop and bought a phone that had pay as you talk facility on it. Jip telephone Judy at the Hill and he explained all what was happening. She advised him that John and Casy with George and Suzie had attended the meeting as they wanted to see Jip and Luci to make sure they were safe! Jip told Judy to convey the message and she told Jip to go along with the set up, as there really was no choice, she also said that there had been no reports of any murders in Bond Street London! Jip's time ran out and they had to purchase another card, but they were so really paranoid at the actions of the police. Jip and Luci were so tired and Jip's eyes were popping out of his face as he struggled to keep alert. Luci started to cry and Jip became strong and he suggested that they have a good nights sleep.

They went in search of the car, but before they found the car they saw across the river bank was a desolate site that had a few buses and a couple of lorries that looked like travellers were there! Jip and Luci headed over to it and as they walked on to the site, a man who introduced himself as Birch greeted them. The man was very Scottish and he had a ginger beard, he said he had met Jip at a festival, a good many years previous. Jip did not remember but the pair had a long yarn and it ended with Birch offering them a truck, where they could sleep and not be disturbed. They gleefully accepted the offer and they were shown a nice clean truck where they found a bed and they both crashed out.It was late into the next day when Jip and Luci came out of the truck. They still were looking rough, Birch saw them and he told them of his girlfriend's house. It was where they headed and they were able to have a bath, Jip was supplied with a pair of jeans, a shirt and a smart looking jumper.

Luci had washed her necessary items, she waited until they had been spun dry then she put on her clean clothes. Birches girlfriend was a really nice person to talk with. She was a very Scottish girl, Luci seemed to get on great with her, and Jip was left to talk with Birch who had taken them there. Jip was well pleased with his information gathering technique, he had discovered about a man who would give them a car and cash for the new B M W motor car. Jip was given all the relevant answers to the tracking down of this man.

Luci had gained a few tips on Scottish witchcraft! They were offered to stay the night at the house and Birch said that he would take them to see the man first thing in the morning. Jip agreed, he had decided to do Birch a favour, by staying. It had meant that Birch had to stay too and he was pleased. Jip and Luci felt relieved and they slept soundly that night. Jip woke at every little noise but he did not disturb anyone.

The next morning was a bright and cold one. Jip and Luci went with Birch to a second hand shop, where they bought themselves a thick jumper and a woolly jacket each.

THE OTHER SIDE OF THE LINE

They were then shown to the car park where the B M W was! It sat there gleaming and Jip then decided that the car was not for sale, he gave Birch fifty quid for his time! Birch would not except fifty so he took away twenty and pushed the thirty back into Jip's pocket. Jip hugged him in a friendly manner and they gave him a lift back to the site. Luci navigated, while Jip drove onto the motorway, they stopped for fuel and for a while they seemed to forget the trouble that they were seemingly in! They flew through Glasgow and were driving along the A62. They drove for about an hour, until Luci apparently saw a sign that read Sam's Boats.

"That's it, turn around!" Luci screamed out.

Jip could not turn until about ten miles later down the road. As they finally headed in a backward direction. Jip was having a, are you sure moment with Luci. It was near to boiling point when Jip also saw the sign and he followed the directions that were written on the sign.
It read,

SAM'S BOATS

Turn left, then second right and follow the hill down.

Jip did as the sign said. They headed down this country lane which ended at a giant hill that fell down to sea level.

Approaching, they saw a boatyard at the bottom. It was full of what looked new Motor Cruisers! Jip pulled the car into the yard and he stopped next to a gleaming Mercedes motor car. Luci looked at Jip and he gave her one of his raw smiles. They stepped out of the car and they both were expecting something to happen, nothing did! Jip gazed around and he felt rather uneasy, he was very wary as he watched a family set off on one of the many, Motor Launches. Jip led Luci over towards the boats and they were startled when a shout of 'oi!' Was aimed at them! They both spun around and they saw an old man who had red hair and a thick beard, he came stumping up to them.

"What business is it of yours that brings you yonder to cross my path?" The old man said in a broad accent.

Jip told the man that they were looking for an owner.

Whose name was Sam. The old man said that it was just the name of the yard, and there was no man ever called Sam! Luci then said about the professor sending them there. The old man suddenly changed and he started treating them as if they were royalties! Jip was impressed, the old man led them to a posh Motor Launch called <u>The Nightingale</u>. The old man then wished them luck and told them he would send one of the workers to teach them about the craft. Jip and Luci climbed aboard the Launch. They first went into the main cabin on the deck where Luci saw a postcard with a picture of Loch Ness on the front of it.

Jip was a believer in the quest for the monster to reveal itself. Luci showed the picture to him.

He took it off her and he read the written side,

To Jip and Luci,

          You are becoming ever nearer with every try,

Things will become clearer with every eye. Take this craft through three locks, two aqueducts, up three

stages, then you will find the figure on the other pages! Then you will have half of the key!

                                                  The Professor.

He turned to Luci and he burst out laughing, Luci thought that he had gone nuts and lost his marbles! Then a young handsome Scottish man who had blond hair disturbed them,

"The boat is full with diesel and all you need to know is in these pages!" The man handed Jip a booklet as he spoke and he left.

Jip opened the booklet to find a set of keys and an introduction to the boat. Jip was brought up in or around the sea and he had knowledge of boats. He still sat and read the instructions and it all came flooding back to him, he started to feel forgetful of their situation and more as if they were on holiday!

When Jip had reached the end section of the booklet, he saw that there was a guide that was headed Loch-Ness Laddie!

He read the guide and it explained the whole route to Loch Ness to him, it was over aqueducts and through locks, it all tallied with the instructions, which were on the note!

"Luci! We are going to Loch Ness!" Jip laughed as he ripped the keys out of the booklet cover.Luci asked him, how had he came to the conclusion and Jip felt rather smart as he explained it all to her. She told him that really it was obvious as the letter had told him all of the information that they needed!

Jip dismissed Luci's remark and he started to investigate the craft.

"Luci! We have gained ourselves a boat!" He shouted as he had gone to the bridge which was undercover on the top deck.

"How long will it take us Jip?" Luci questioned.

Jip told her to expect a journey of around two to three days, she seemed happy with this and she went to the Kitchen (Galley) area of the boat. She saw that all the provisions were there and that it was all vegetarian food! She ran to Jip and she explained her anxiety of feeling like she was being watched all of the time. Jip said that he felt the same.

He again stated to her that doing this was better that being in prison and she seemed again to agree. Jip started the boat engines and it started thudding in a very quiet manner. Jip revved the engine, he felt the boat start to pull. He shouted to Luci to undo the ropes that were tying in to its berth, she managed to do it, and leap back onto the boat as Jip manoeuvred the craft. He safely piloted the craft into the middle of the canal. The canal linked the boat yard with the Moray Firth, which was filled by the North Sea.

THE OTHER SIDE OF THE LINE

CHAPTER SEVENTEEN

The morning after, Jip and Luci's disappearance was a good one for the ministers. It was because the opposition leaders had been involved in a crime and had run away!
The real truth was that it all was an elaborate plan of the police! It was so that the government could issue the go ahead of section 48 without the interference from any opposition. It was devious and underhanded! It had been thought that seeing Jip was fairly intelligent, he would find the car keys and go on the set quest, it was deemed that the time he would end up at Loch Ness, would be long enough for the ministers to create the unopposed section 48 a reality!
"Perfect" One sinister minister was overheard saying.
Of course Jip and Luci were running scared, as any normal person would have been!
Back at the Hill, everyone had been huddled in their benders or tree houses, as the weather had been bad with rain and gales for the last two days. Casy had been clever enough to have tethered his Horses before he and John had left for London, under the tree where he had built his home. Judy was living in the site office as the terencial rain had flooded her bender and she was keeping the show going. Dave was still in the prison. Alex and Elaine had not been seen for days.John and Casy had jumped into George's car with Suzie, George hadto return to London and go back to the oilrigs, and this was a great excuse for them all to travel free!In London George had dropped off the three at the Rainbow centre in Kentish Town. They had arrived the day that Jip and Luci had disappeared. The local paper that they found hanging on a notice board had said how the opposition leaders had failed to attend the second day and John was furious! Casy calmed him after telephoning Judy, who had explained the reasons to him. John and Casy with Suzie all attended the meeting the next day, they had managed to gather around 400 of their friends or colleagues to walk to the building with them.

THE OTHER SIDE OF THE LINE

It was just to show the ministers that the Hill was backed by everyone concerned!
Ten am the next morning, everyone had arrived at the centre and banners that they had used before, which had been left at the rainbow centre were brought out again. They walked the three miles to
Downing Street to protest about the treatment of the case, they were three days late but it had an effectual ending.
Someone somewhere had leaked a file, which had abated the people of the Hill to be unwashed peasants who were undesirable to society! Amongst the bad news, there was a bright feeling as when the papers did break the news, they told of a peaceful rally and it praised the commitment of the people. Jip and Luci would have been proud of their friends as the review was halted, so that John and Casy's solicitors could have time to prepare the case.
The ministers thought that the plan had not worked, so they decided it would be better to have an open enquiry of the environmental changes that would effect the Hill. They thought that they would announce the Jip and Luci affair as unreliable personnel who had used the system to give them a holiday at Loch Ness!
The ministers had not taken into account that Jip and Luci had friends who actually knew that it was a set up! They had not mentioned it before as none of them had heard anyone ask about them. The meeting was arranged to take place in the debate room at number three Downing Street. It had been set back to start two weeks from that date. John and Casy were pleased and they could not wait to tell Jip or Luci. They contacted Judy at the Hill and conveyed the message. Judy had spent the day frantically trying to track Jip and Luci down, she had been given the number of their new phone, but she was unable to get any reply!
Jip and Luci had been on the Moray Firth for two and a half days and time had flown by them!
They had arrived at a place that was called Drumnadrochit, it was where a great castle sat.

THE OTHER SIDE OF THE LINE

In the pages it had stated that the Nightingale was able to berth there overnight. Jip had docked the boat and they had found a pub near by and they were enjoying a drink! Luci had mentioned to Jip that she had wanted to contact Judy, Jip had told her that they should not use the land telephone, as it would be bugged! Luci did not agree! She wondered off and she found a quaint cottage, which had a wire coming off of it, she decided to ask the owners if there was a telephone anywhere around. She found a very old Scottish woman who invited her in and she told Luci that she had one of the two telephones that was in the village! Luci asked if she might use it, she was told it was a pay phone and she did not have any change! She would have to go back to the pub, she was worried because she did not want Jip to find out she was using the land line telephone. Luci then trudged back to the pub and she told Jip that she needed to use the toilet and as she did she asked the barmaid if she could have change for the electricity meter that was on the boat! When she returned the woman gave her change for a five-pound English bank note. Jip did not notice Luci getting the change as he was talking with an old Scots man who was telling him the tale of Loch Ness. Luci then asked Jip if he minded if she took a walk and he said for her not to go too far!

When she had returned to the old woman, she used the telephone and Judy told her of the delayed review and she stated that Jip and her would have to clear their names! Casy was planning to help them while John held up the press! Luci was elated and she told Judy that they were going to try and get back, this was so Jip could find Casy and John and create a way out of the situation!

Luci thanked the old woman that offered her a drink, she had refused and she ran back to the public house. She found Jip playing the piano and he seemed to be singing a duet with the old Scots man! Luci could not make any sense out of the Scottish mans singing and she bought a drink and sat and listened anyway. Jip started to make up a song and the man gave him the stage as he went to the toilet!

THE OTHER SIDE OF THE LINE

Jip sang,

> Where are we headed to
> What are the ways?
> Anciantical ways of madness
> To the bright kind of play.
>
> Mystical surroundings playing away
> Happy meandering the order of the day
>
> Isn't it a wonderful beginning, all around I feel safe?
> Eating mystical meandering which is pleasant to taste
> Oh, beautiful surroundings you have blended my mystical belief
> You have blended the matter as a flower grows from a leaf.

Jip finished playing and singing in a classical way, nobody clapped or gave him any encouragement so he went to see Luci. Luci asked if they could sit outside, she had something that she wanted to discuss with him. They both went with their drinks and sat on a wooden table, it was drizzling and Jip did not seem to mind, or Luci! She explained the plan and Jip agreed that it would be right to try and prove that they were innocent.
"The police will be watching the Hill though!" Jip explained to her.
Luci did not give up, she told Jip that he could wear a wig and some glasses, maybe grow a beard!
Jip then said,
"Do we find the professor or should we let him find us!"
They did not speak for a while as they finished their drinks and they went back to the Launch. The sky had started to pull its dark veil over the evening and it was nice to see all of the other boats that were there all lit up. Jip entered the main deck and he sat staring out at the glistening water. He watched as another boat similar to the one they were on, come and dock close to where Jip had berthed.

It looked like a party was going on! He was stunned to see men and woman taking off their clothes and diving into the water! The noise that they started making alerted Luci to the main deck; she looked at Jip in a stern way. Jip got up and went into the bridge area and he started the engines, Luci took this as a hint to untie the ropes and she did just that. Jip turned the craft one hundred and eighty degrees and they were underway.
"How far was that town we past?" Jip said to her.
"It was about three hours and the time now is eleven o'clock captain!" Luci replied in a buoyant way?
Luci found the pages and she went to the section that had a map on the page. She was studying it and when she found what she was looking for she said,
"Here it is! Fort Augustus!"
She explained to Jip that it was not too far. Four hours later it took!
Jip was the first to spot car headlights in the distance and he tooted the foghorn as he read a sign that read Fort Augustus speed limit 2 knots. Jip slowed the craft accordingly and he saw a bank where he could moor the boat up. He struggled to see, until he found a switch that lit up the river in front of him! Luci looked for any luggage they had left.

All she found was two pairs of Jip's socks and some of her things. Jip noticed, as they grew closer that there was a slipway and he said, "That is where we will leave this beauty!"

"Aye, Aye!" Luci said as she again staggered up to the front bow of the boat. She grabbed the rope and was waiting until Jip had steered the craft in closer until she tied the rope to a hook that she saw.

It did not take very long and they were moored onto the slipway and Jip had left the keys in the ignition, turned off. The pair stepped down off the boat and they started to walk wearily into the town. It was really dark and when he checked his watch, he saw it was indeed six o'clock in the morning! By the time they had found the town centre they were tired, but the will to get away from the boat overwhelmed them and kept them going! They were lucky as they found a café that was just opening its doors, they entered and ordered their usual drinks as Jip checked the money situation. He was impressed as he still had over seven hundred pounds in the envelope! Jip sat drinking his drink and he gazed out into the street through the glass front pane. He thought of how they were to travel and he saw a sign advertising cheap cars! Jip made his mind up, they would buy a used car and along the way they would find a city which had a fancy dress shop. There they would purchase the necessary items that they would require to fool the police if they were watching the Hill, as they expected. Luci finished her food first and once Jip had finished, the pair of them paid the bill and walked to find the car sales place.

They followed the direction on the sign and it led them down an alleyway to a set of converted garages. Jip went inside the open one. Luci did not like garages, so she hung about outside. When Jip entered he had found a very hungover looking man sat drinking a hot drink!

"Any decent motors mate?" Jip inquired.

The man lazily pointed his hand to a door that was at the end of the workshop.

"All I have is out back mate!" The man said.
Jip went through the door and he saw three cars, one was a new Granada, which had no wheels and the second was a Lada! Jip then decided straight away that he would have to take the Fiat x1/9 that was the only clean looking one of the three. He opened the door and he struggled to get in, the keys had been left in the ignition, so he tried to start it. The man came out and in his hands he had a rotor arm,
"It wont go without this" The man chuckled.
Jip asked him how much he wanted and the man said he could take it for £350! Jip asked him if it had any papers and he was shown a MOT certificate that had about two months on it and a log book, the man had fitted the rotor arm into the distributor and the engine fire up with no problem. Jip drove the car fast at the wall and he slammed the brakes on! They worked fine! Jip told the man that he would take it and he went out to ask Luci for the money. He did not tell her what he was buying; yet she really did not care. The deal was then settled and they were soon on their way. Jip went straight to a petrol station and filled the car tank. Then they drove the motorway after joining it at Glasgow. Luci found that even the radio worked and the music seemed to be to her liking as she started joining in with the songs that were playing! Jip pulled off the motorway near Leeds and he went and bought a beard and a wig, then he went to an optician and he purchased a pair of trendy tinted spectacles.
Soon they were back on the road and as they approached Wrexham, Jip put on his disguise. Luci had bought a wig as well and she was now dark black in her hair colour. Jip thought she looked terrific but he did not tell her as not to offend her. It took them about two hours to reach Valleydale.
Jip drove to the back end of town and he dumped the car at Creach's quarry, they walked over country to the Hill and when they did arrive they were shattered! They stayed in Johns Tree house, as they knew that he was still in London.

THE OTHER SIDE OF THE LINE

They did not want to be seen near the bus yet!
The pair of them slept for a whole day and night.

CHAPTER EIGHTEEN

Judy was the first person to see that someone was in Casy's tree house and she had taken a peek. Her bender was very close by. When she woke the next morning she went to the site office as usual. While she was there, Casy had telephoned from London and she was able tell him the news! She noticed that the police had set up some form of roadblock as she had first arrived, she conveyed this to Casy who in turn informed John who was with him. They told Judy that they were hitch hiking back from London, that very moment and they suggested that they might get home before mid-night!

Judy decided that she would find out from Elaine, why the police were crawling over the village. She was shocked when Elaine had told her that Alex had told her that they had shot two gay men! Judy would not believe her and Elaine stated that it was a under cover rumour,

"Elaine if it was under cover then why are all the police hanging around the streets?" Judy questioned her.

"I was told that they were running away from the murder!" Elaine shook as she spoke.Judy dismissed her as an old bag! She knew that Jip had never ever been the slightest bit interested in guns! She was sure he hated anything to do with them and this told her that it must be some kind of set up! Judy casually strolled back to the site office and she started to ring around London, to find any information she could.

It was about five o'clock when a vanload of police started to search Jip and Luci's bus for them. Judy felt helpless, but the people of the Hill all congregated around the bus and they chanted them away! The police were not happy and they all were extremely serious. Judy had to admit that she was frightened

for her safety for a moment or two!When Casy and John appeared the excitement had all died down.

Judy had made a fire under Casy's tree house and that was where the two had found her. She made them a drink and she asked them, "Where is Suzie?"

The boys explained that she had seen her auntie and that she was staying at her house in London, they told her that Jip could stay there with them when they go to London as planned. Judy was happy, she was able at last to speak about the murders, and she had exactly the same reactions from the boys as she had.

"I am personally going to clear their names!" Casy said positively.

John vowed to do the same and they all made a pact. Then they all went to their homes. Casy joined John in his bender and John told him to sleep in his bed, while he left and went and slept in Suzie's bender, he was missing her a great deal.

The next morning, Judy had woke early as someone had shouted into all of the benders, that the police were again at Jip and Luci's bus! They were not there when John and Casy arrived. Jip had heard the commotion and he was awake sat looking out from the built in window across the Hill, he was pleased to watch people caring for them. He was annoyed that he could not get to his bus yet! He decided that he would take one of Casy's Horses to ride to the bus. He rode to the office and there were shouts of;

'We love you, and don't let them get you down!'

He rode along the site, he felt like he was king of the Hill! People were bowing in front of the Horse, most of all though, Jip saw the smiling faces. Once Jip had reached his bus, he saw Casy emerge, seeing Jip on one of his Horses he laughed,

"Change places more often dear chap?"

That statement seemed to break the ice, Jip leapt down from the Horse and he went into his bus. Everything was a mess as the police had obviously searched it and all of his papers and clothes were strewn everywhere. Jip decided then that he was not allowing this to happen again! Casy was pessimistic at the statement and he started to help Jip clean up.

John had seen Jip enter his bus and he had seen one of the teenage boys and gave him a pound. It was for him to keep an eye out at the bridge for the police! John gave the boy a mobile telephone from the office and he told him.

"Any sign of the police near to the bridge then hide and telephone the office, just hit the redial button!"

The young boy told him he knew how a telephone worked and he gathered a few other children and they took their fishing rods so that they could fish from the bridge.

Luci arrived later and she did not see the initial mess and Jip decided that it was best not to tell her.

She lit the burner and made hot drinks for Jip and Casy. John then entered and he told them of his look out boys! Jip was glad that he had friends. Luci went to the site office with Judy and she was there when the boy had telephoned to say that Alex was on his way up! Luci ran and told Jip and when he appeared. Casy was sat in the bus while Jip and Luci were behind it having gone out the driver's door. Alex asked if Casy had seen them and he told him that the meeting that was planned in London was changed! He said that the ministers are looking into the true facts of Jip and Luci's custody, it was Alex's belief that the police had slipped up somewhere in the investigation and he told Casy that no bodies had been found to substantiate the rumour of two gay men being shot! He agreed with Casy as he told him that he did not believe the story anyway! Alex said he had written to the ministers. He was asking for an inquiry into the police's handling of the Valleydale affairs, it was a stroke of luck that one of the ministers involved was a old friend of his.

He had spoke with him for a few hours the day before. Alex left.

Casy told Jip and Luci of the new meeting! Jip was relieved and Luci was too. Casy asked Jip if he was still interested in finding out the truth about the shootings, he suggested that the pair take Jip's motorcycle and go to London and find the truth out themselves!

Jip told Casy that he would think about it.

He was worried that he would be arrested again if he were seen! Casy said that his plan would mean that they both wore disguises and that it would illuminate them from any harm. Jip still stated that he wanted to think it over and the conversation was dropped. Luci made some tea and there was yet another scare as the boy rang John and said that a police van was parked down near to the bridge. Jip and Casy decided to take a look from a distance, he went and fetched his other Horse, they both rode off around the Hill. When they caught site of the police van they watched it for around ten minutes. The van then seemed to be prompted by them, it left and Jip and Casy shook each other's hands. Then they went back to the bus and they ate a hearty vegetarian feast that Luci had cooked. John was there and as he ate he said of how he too wanted to go to London to see Suzie. Jip explained to him that they were thinking of taking the motorcycle, as it would mean they could travel easier and faster! John agreed and he said that he needed a car. Jip then remembered the Fiat that he had hidden at the Quarry and he suggested that John should use it to get Suzie. John thought it was a good idea, he agreed that he would fetch the car and bring it to the Hill. Jip told him not too! He stated that he did not want the police to know he was back and the car could give them away! John realised and he said that if they all left on the Sunday, then they would have five days before the meeting, this would give them time to find out the truth about the men who Jip was sure were dead!
The night was a calm one and everyone slept without disturbance.
The next two days were blustery cold winter's days.
Jip saw no one for the two days and it was not until Casy turned up on the Sunday that they saw anyone! Casy told Jip his plan, he stated that they would ride to London by motorcycle and they would stay at Suzie's aunts, they would visit the house in Bond Street and also attend the meeting, they would wear a disguise so that they would not be recognised.
Jip and Luci agreed and they had an early night to ready Jip for the long motorcycle ride the next morning.

THE OTHER SIDE OF THE LINE

The next morning was soon to arrive and the weather was still blustery. Jip took the motorcycle down to the café; it was so he was able to check it over under a tarpaulin. John came over and Jip gave him the keys to the Fiat. He left and said he would meet them at Suzie's aunt's house and he gave Jip the address.

After he had checked the bike, Jip went and found Casy who was mustering up some waterproof clothing, which he managed successfully to do. Jip then rode the bike to his bus and went and said his goodbye to Luci,

"I've got to go, I need to clear our names, you know this is true love" He told her, then they had a long deep kiss.

It did not take long before they had joined the motorway; they only stopped once along the way, as they were so wet they had to get dried in a service station! It was about two o'clock in the afternoon when they finally arrived at Suzie's Aunt's. Casy was pleased as he saw his loved one. John arrived about an hour later; they all enjoyed warmth, and some tea. A night of talking the next day's events over was had.

The next morning was an early one for Jip as Luci telephoned him at eight in the morning! She pleaded with him for her to join him! Jip explained that it would be too dangerous as the police knew them as a couple and they would not expect him to be there on his own. Luci finally understood and she wished him a lot of luck.

Casy did not awake until later and once he had.He was treated with the others to a giant breakfast cooked by Suzie's aunt. Then the plan was put into action!

John and Jip took the tube train, Casy took the bus and they all met in a café near to Bond Street. After a coffee the three all wearing disguises walked up Bond street and Jip pointed out the house, they saw a sign on the door panel that read,

No admittance, passes to be shown at all times!

Jip felt uneasy, he was still sure he had seen the bodies of two men who had been shot!

He quivered as they walked passed the house.

Jip then took the boys on a guided tour of the garages and they left soon afterwards. They went to a local public house and sat drinking, Jip explained about the Colonel and Todge, he mentioned that he knew he was set up by the police, but he did not understand the Colonel and Todge fiasco! Casy then suggested that the best way of finding this out was to approach the house that scared Jip! Casy arranged it all, he said that if Jip rode the bike, he would walk up to the house and find out the truth! Jip said he did not mind waiting at the end of the street, so it was arranged. This time Jip and Casy took the bus while John took the tube train.

After a lunch at Suzie's aunt's house, Jip and Casy headed off, John went to Brixton to gather support for the meeting, and Suzie went with him. Jip drove the bike to the corner of Bond Street, Casy left his crash helmet with Jip and he started walking up the street. Jip watched as Casy entered the grounds of the house.

Casy walked boldly up to the front door and he rang the chime, it was a pretty little song it played. A woman with a stern face greeted him, "What can I do for you?" She asked.

"I am trying to find The Colonel or Todge!" Casy announced blatantly.

"They are not here! You can if you want leave a message!" The woman sounded militant to Casy as she spoke.

Casy told her that he would call back at a later date. He apologised for any inconvenience he had caused! As he said that, a black limousine pulled up and Casy dashed out! He saw as the doors opened, there were two men, and one had blond hair while the other man was small in height. Casy walked at a pace passed them, they did not take any notice of him. It was as he reached Jip's bike that he saw two police cars go racing up to the house. Jip also saw the two men and as soon as he saw the police cars he started the engine and drove to Casy and they were soon racing back to where they were staying. The two of them were very tired when they returned and they did not discuss the days outing before bed that night.

Jip telephoned Luci and they spoke for about two hours and Jip gave thirty pounds to Suzie's aunt as a thank you for letting them stay!
The next morning and Jip had his early wake up call again from Luci, this morning Casy joined Jip early as he stated that he was unable to settle that night for thinking of the blond fellow. They discussed the topic and Jip realised that the men Casy had seen had to be the two who were shot! Casy remarked that they had recovered very quickly! Jip finally laughed aloud and he was then sure that it was all a trick to get him away from the meeting!
"It back fired on them!" John announced as he overheard the conversation,
"How do we confirm all of this and to who?" Casy asked them all.
Jip said that the only way would be to get pictures of the men and go to the press and explain it all to them!
"That will be hard to do, I reckon that we should tell the press the truth and let them get the evidence!" Suzie said as she arrived.
The telephone then started to ring and it was passed to Jip, on the line was Jip's friend Nick. He explained that he had organised the rally for the meeting that was the next day.
He told Jip that he would like to iron out the finer points. They arranged to meet and have lunch. Casy and Suzie said they would go over to Bond Street and watch for anything that could be of help!
Jip and John took the car as it was pouring with rain. They drove over to Brixton.
They arrived at Brixton and met up with Nick, he was in his lorry and Jip was surprised to see a couple of coaches and more vans all parked in the grounds. They hid the car amongst the lorries and they entered the church with Nick.
Once inside, Nick said he would supply them with a couple of suits for the boys to wear at the meeting. Jip thought it was hilarious, as he had never wore a suit in his life! John asked for a suit for Casy and Nick said that he would see what he could do! Jip explained that Alex had informed them that the meeting had changed.

There was to be a debate on him and Luci! Nick explained that that meeting was not the one that was happening the next day, but was arranged for the following month! Jip asked what the meeting was to be about and he was told it was a review of the people's fight against Section 48! He told Jip that a lot of solicitors for different people would be attending and that it was a very formal gathering with a lot of press. John agreed with Jip that this could possibly be the publicity they needed and they all agreed to meet the next morning early as the opening was to be at ten in the morning. Jip thanked Nick and they arranged to see him at his grandfather's house at eight that evening to pick up the three suites.

John and Jip then left and went back to the house, Suzie and Casy were sat waiting and they told Jip that they had seen who they suspected were the Colonel and Todge appear at the house! Casy described how they looked and Jip agreed that it must have been them, he was nervous because he knew that they would definitely be at the meeting!

Jip telephoned Luci while the others all pitched in and cooked the food.

After all of the excitement of the day, Casy and Jip with John all caught a tube train to Shepherds Bush where Nick met them and took them to his grandfathers house. Inside they were all presented with a clean suite! Casy's been greying pinstriped while Johns and Jip's were dark blue. They could not try them on there, as Nick's grandfather was ill and he needed his sleep, they all carried their borrowed clothes back to the house. It was fairly late when they returned so they all crashed out, so that they would be fit for the early morning call!

CHAPTER NINETEEN

The morning was an early one, Luci again woke Jip up at the crack of dawn and they talked for about an hour. It was amusing that Casy had woken up and he had put on his borrowed suit! Jip had never seen him look so clean, he had even had a shave! Jip went and he dressed himself in his borrowed suit and he had trouble in finding his false beard to wear, John appeared all really smartly dressed and he too wore a false beard. Jip appeared after a while and they all burst out giggling as they all realised that none of them had any shoes and they all had to wear their boots under their suits! It was decided that with the trousers over the top of the boots no one would be able to notice! Jip took a gaze out of the window, it was raining and blowing a gale again. John suggested that they should hire a taxi and they ordered one for nine o'clock.
The meeting was taking place at Westminster and the taxi cost them twenty-five pounds to get them there!
As they stepped from the Taxi, a mountain of steps faced them,
"Are you ready for this?" Casy asked Jip.
He nodded and he cringed, he was very nervous but he felt the Hill needed him there!
They walked the steps and found them being searched by two security men at the entrance, it was just a small pat over.
Then they were asked to walk through a detector gate and Jip was stopped and asked to empty his pockets, it was his bike keys that had sent the beeper beeping. Once that was over Jip found the toilet.
He dashed around his eyes with water and he placed in some coloured contact lenses that Casy had bought the day before. He was nearly physically sick with nerves, pulling himself together he went and joined the others. Casy had seen the refreshment room and he led the two there. They sat and enjoyed a refreshing peppermint tea and Jip and Casy both had a smoke. Jip saw there was no ashtray so he instinctively went to another table.

He asked one of the two men sat if they minded if he borrowed the ash try! He had such a fright! The man who turned and faced him was Todge! Luckily he did not stare long at this bearded hippie! Jip actually found him polite as he passed him one of the two ashtrays that were on the table. Jip felt relieved as he said thank you and returned to his seat. Casy sensed that something had happened and he prompted Jip to tell him.

"Dodgy company!" Jip whispered.

Casy wondered his eyes around the room as he sipped his peppermint tea. He saw the two men and he confirmed that they were the two men he had seen at Bond Street. Jip then felt more intense with the situation, he rushed his tea and hinted to everyone that he was feeling uncomfortable. John was first to finish his tea and he stood up, so did Casy and the two flanked Jip out into the lobby. Casy noticed that the Colonel and Todge never even looked as the three passed their table. In the lobby, the boys found the listing board and found the room, it was Room one! They looked to find out where it was, after a short expedition of wrong turns!They entered room one and they saw that there was quite a lot of people who were already there, Jip saw a few faces that he knew, he did not let on though.

Jip then sat on a chair at the rear of the room and Casy and John joined him. They stared around the room. Jip classed it as a hall as he could see a stage, which had three desks with four seats on it, each seat was linked to a microphone, it looked very court like to him. A man then sat next to Casy and he introduced himself as Jordan, he said he worked for a leading newspaper and was there to cover the event.

John then started pointing out all of the barristers and solicitors that were there on the behalf of the Hill! Jip was impressed as they all looked as if they were ready for business!

It was not very long before the usher entered and she instructed for everyone to take a seat, she ordered the press camera's to the front around the sides.

She positioned the for and against solicitors into a left and right side congregation. Jip and the others stayed seated to the left at the back of the big room. The ministers then arrived on the stage and the usher formally introduced them,

"The Right Honourable Secretary of State Highways" She introduced the first.

Jip remembered that he had put the petition into this mans hands. The others were introduced as his understudies and the meeting was opened.

The agenda was opened with the question from one of the barristers, "Why was section 48 given priority before the public?"

The answer was short and straight to the point.

"It was published and made available for the public!"

"Yes minister but who had known about it?" Came a fiery question from the same solicitor.

"All the local councils were made to take a vote and the vote was a yes vote!" The minister did not seem to be perturbed at the line of questioning.

The debate went on for quite a while and by lunch they still had not admitted that section 48 was a mistake!

Jip, Casy and John all listened at every bit of the suggestions and it was nerve racking when Jip's name was raised over the protesting of section 48. Jip was pleased that there was no mention of them and the Bond street affair.Lunch was a break and the afternoon's session was a lively affair! A big row broke out over the scape goat attitudes that the minister was trying to use! A statement that stayed in everyone's mind was one by an older man, who said,

"My honourable friend, we are dismayed at the way the whole operation has failed, I vote for a re-think on the whole sordid affair!"

The answer was to astound everyone.

"We believed we acted honestly if not a little hastily. The urgency of this problem we believe, is the solution already been proven, section 48 must go ahead!"

The usher then closed the meeting for the day and Jip, Casy and John were the first to leave and a sharp dressed woman followed them. When they reached the bottom of the steps she ran after them and she asked,
"Can you tell me if there is any truth in the two protesters who used governments money to have a holiday in Scotland?"
Jip looked at John. John told the woman that they had knowledge but they would have to meet later as they just wanted to get as far away as possible. They were all angry at the minister's stand! The woman said she would meet them all at the Phoenix inn, it was in Kensington and very plush. They agreed that they would meet her there at around nine o'clock that evening. The three then went to the tube and they caught a tube and a taxi back to the house.
Suzie asked them of how it all went and the mixed reviews shocked her.
"Are they going to go ahead with section 48?" She questioned them all.
Jip said that he thought that they really did not stand much of a chance, not by the way the minister closed the meeting!
Jip then went and he telephoned Luci. She told him that she had heard a review on the radio and that it did not seem to be positive and they said that the fight is the public verses the government! Jip felt the same. When the time arrived to meet the woman, they all dressed again in the disguises, they squeezed in to the Fiat and drove over to Kensington. Jip felt strange as they entered and went to the reception desk,
"We are to meet a Miss Massy?" Jip said.
The waiter instructed them that table 48 had been reserved for them! Jip thought it was a nice touch that the number was 48! Sitting at the table was the young woman who stood and greeted them as they joined her.
"Good to see you again" She said politely.
They ordered food and after the meal that was delicious.

THE OTHER SIDE OF THE LINE

They started to get down to business.

"Jip and Luci are still wanted by the police? They have evaded capture since June this year? I have been told that they hid in Scotland using stolen Government money!" The woman was blunt as she spoke.

Jip thought that she made him and Luci out to be terrorists! Jip did not like it and he explained the whole true event from day one to her! It must have taken an hour and it stopped when she asked,

"How do you know all of this?"

Jip jumped out of his seat and he ripped off his disguise and he revealed himself!

The woman stayed really calm and she shook his hand in a friendly manner. Casy left to use the toilet when he returned he saw that there were four plain-clothes policemen approaching the table!

"Quick run! It's a trap!" Casy screamed as he ran towards the men. Casy blocked the policemen's path!

Jip ran out into the kitchen and he saw a door facing the outside, he ran through it to find himself on a fire escape ladder! He saw that there were two officers down at the bottom, Jip panicked! He saw a washing line, it was tied to a post. Jip jumped across the escape to the wire and he grabbed it only for it to snap! It sent him reeling to the floor! He had twisted his ankle and he struggled to get out of the garden he was in. He limped down the little alley to find another restaurant and he limped through the restaurant and he walked through to its kitchen! He startled the workers as he limped as fast as he could out into the street. He heard the sound of police car sirens and he ran for his life! He was looking for a tube station but he could not see one! He sat in a dark alley, which was near to the canal. He waited until the lights disappeared and he found a bus stop and he jumped on a bus, the bus went in the opposite direction that he wanted and he jumped off when he recognised he was in or near to Chelsea bridge!

THE OTHER SIDE OF THE LINE

Jip limped down to the river and he walked along a subway and getting to the end he saw a set of railings, he clambered over them and sat on the riverbank. He felt scared and his fear heightened when he saw the lights of a helicopter coming up the river, he then heard sirens and a lot of tyres squealing! He was doomed as the helicopter shone the light right on him and as he tried to escape about five policemen clambered over the fence towards him, they caught him with a rugby tackle and they were punching him as they held him down. Then he was thrown into a police launch, he hit his head and lost consciousness for a minute! He endured about five kicks to his body as he was taken across the river! Jip also had blood rushing from a wound that was on his leg, the police just grabbed him as if he was a piece of meat and they dragged him on his back up the steps to a waiting police van! He was then taken at speed to West End Central police station, where he was thrown into a cell that was fit for a rodent to live in! He lay out onto the cell bench, he was in extreme pain as his leg and ankle was in a terrible state! He really needed a doctor, but Casy and John joined him instead!

"Are you alright Jip" Casy kindly asked.

Jip told him his story and they all helped with each other's wounds. They stayed there for two hours until a policeman opened the hatch and he said,

"You boys, are in a lot of trouble, we are waiting for the warrants to arrive and then you will not pass go! Prepare yourselves for a journey!"

Jip asked for a drink and they all received a glass of water each, well it was a plastic cup. Two more hours passed and Jip knew that they were in for a little stay! Six big uniformed officers came into the cell and they physically removed the three men, they all had to wear handcuffs and they took them to a locked room. There they waited another twenty minutes until the door opened and Todge entered! He carried a folder and he stated, with a distingtive look in his eyes and a smile half on his face.

"Here are the warrants, I want you all to follow me to the desk sergeant so that he can release you into my custody!"
Jip moved first and they all went to the front desk where the sergeant was waiting. The boys did not realise that they were being placed into Government control and all Jip could think of was the beautiful cottage and he relaxed a little, he believed that they were on the way to the cottage! He did not read the letter that he had to sign as he was so confident, he told the others to follow suite and they did all sign.
Then they were placed back into the interview room and they were fed, it tasted like over boiled vegetables. Then they were ushered back to the dirty cell. They were left with their handcuffs on and it was extremely uncomfortable for them all. Another hour or so passed and by now the three were feeling very tired and as they had just all fallen to sleep they were woke up! Around five or six burly police officers filled the cell and from behind them came the Colonel and Todge, "Time for you to join us!"
The Colonel said and Jip saw that snarl he called a grin.
Casy was handcuffed to Jip while John who still had a sore shoulder was led on his own. They were led out of the station and into a yard where a white van was waiting, they were bundled into the back of the van. They found that the van did not have any windows! It only had wooden seats for them to sit on!Feeling tired Jip slept, Casy could not sleep and neither could John. They just sat totally annoyed at the situation that they were in. They both were negative in their thinking. The journey took them three hours and they ended up at Southampton docks! The Colonel and his guards released the three from the back of the van. They all stood bleary eyed at the harbour.
"Welcome to your new homes!" The Colonel said.
The Colonel pointed into the sea and Jip was frightened, all he could see was dark water! He convinced himself that they were going to be thrown into the freezing water and never seen again!
He was even more convinced when they were ordered to walk down the steps, which led to the sea. At the bottom was a steel clad boat!

It looked like something out of Mad Max! John thought. Casy was on the same trip as Jip and no one spoke as they clambered onto the metal boat. They were told to climb into a hole which led them to a room which was pure metal, on the side of the hull there was a metal bar, which the men were handcuffed to, it had been especially welded there for that job! Soon enough the boat began to move and the three men resigned themselves to being wet as they all were convinced that they were going to be thrown into the sea! The three heard a loud clanging noise and the hold where they sat was opened from above,
"Come on get them out!" Todge shouted to a guard as he undid the handcuffs.
The three climbed one by one onto the deck of the small boat and they saw that they were against the hull of a big ship!
"Any last requests?" Todge teased them.
Jip shock his head, Casy pleaded to go home but he was pushed and told to shut up! John stayed calm, he knew he could swim well and he was preparing himself mentally for the swim he thought he had to face.
The Colonel led the three onto a set of rusty steps and once they had climbed them they found themselves on a massive ship!
"It's a bloody prison ship!" Jip suddenly said as he realised what they were on.
"Wow! Aren't you very clever! This ship is twenty miles from the shore and it is manned day and night, I hope you won't get seasick!" Todge was laughing as he finished his statement.

CHAPTER TWENTY

Luci was waiting in the bus with Judy, they were discussing a letter that had arrived that day. They had no idea of the mess that Jip and the others had got into! The girls were panicking over the letter that said a group of legal representatives were to visit the next day and the letter said everyone would be interviewed!
The Hill was still teaming with people and a happy atmosphere was abounded. Judy was staying at the bus with Luci while the men were away and it was ironic that the pair was awake at that time of morning. It was not long before they had had a drink and gone back to sleep!
The next morning at about mid-day Luci telephoned Suzie, she explained that the boys had gone to meet a female reporter and they had not returned! Luci trusted Jip but Judy was a little fussed over John! The girls had a feeling something had happened that was not good! Then a group of smartly dressed people entered the site and introduced themselves as the legal representatives for the Hill. Judy was telephoning all over London trying to track down the three men. Luci had thought that they might have been on their way home but she realised it was a bit late in the day as London was only four hours away! Jed came to the office and he stated that they had to find Jip and Casy as the legal representatives were asking all kinds of questions and the people of the Hill wanted a representative all of their own! He joined Judy in tracking down the men, but he drew a blank as well. Luci said she would speak to Alex, as he must have an idea to where the men were! Everyone agreed with her and they all sat listening as she telephoned the library. Elaine told Luci that Alex was in London, she would ask him as soon as she had seen him. Luci ran to bus in tears, she was frightened for Jip!
Judy joined her and she burst out all of her emotions as well.
After a while the two women came to their senses and Luci said,

THE OTHER SIDE OF THE LINE

"It will soon be the winter solstice?"
Judy replied that it would have been the first with John and they started to cry again.
That went on all of the evening and Luci cried herself to sleep. The two girls woke early the next day and they were dashed with hope when they heard Jip's motorcycle turn up! Alas! Luci was so disappointed as she saw it was Suzie who had ridden it back!
The girls all discussed everything in the bus and it was decided that they would all put a brave face on and they would organise a solstice party!
The three women walked across the site. They went to the café where they told Joe about the plans, he said they could use the stage and the café for the venue and Luci who could not think straight asked him if he could get somebody to make up some flyers! He said it was no problem at all and he went about doing it. Luci was getting more and more distraught and she cracked and told the two other women,
"Let us drive down and pester Elaine!"
Judy was first to agree and Suzie who was tired said she had to sleep and she went to her bender. Luci went to the site office and grabbed the LandRover keys; she met Judy at the LandRover. Luci drove to the library and the brakes squealed as she did. They parked outside the library and they both entered.
Elaine seemed pleased to see them and she said that Alex was on his way home and he had some information on the whereabouts of the men! The girls were asked to meet at the Valleydale arms that very evening at seven o'clock. This was at last something to look forward too!
The two then left and they drove to the waterfalls where they sat peacefully watching the fall of the water.
Luci told Judy that Jip had brought her their many times before, she even told Judy about the time they made love in the water! Judy did not really listen as she too was missing her loved one. As Luci went on about Jip, Judy had heard enough,

"Luci, lets organise the solstice party and stop all of this moping around!"

That did it! Luci ran to the LandRover and she started the engine, Judy leapt in and they drove across the fields back onto the Hill. Not another word was spoke until they had arrived back at the bus. Luci realised she must have been going on a bit and she apologised to Judy. The two women spent the rest of the afternoon making leaflets and they did manage to avoid speaking with the legal people! Then after some tea they drove to the Valleydale Arms the local public house.

Elaine had saved them a table and she told them that she had found out that Alex was a married man and had children! This was entertaining to the women and they had a good yarn until Alex walked in.

He walked over to them all with a briefcase in his hand and he sat down, he stared at the two women,

"I am afraid that the Government have arrested Jip, Casy and John for the London affair! I have tried to find out where they are being held but as yet I have been unsuccessful! I am working on that!" Alex was quite formal as he spoke.

The conversation went on for about an hour and once the women were sure that Alex could not tell them anymore. He promised that he would find out and the women left him to sort out his problem with Elaine. The women drove back to the Hill. The evening was then finished off with Judy and Luci both sat discussing the prison that they most likely expected Jip and John to be in. Suzie arrived later and she was told the news.

The next day was a wet and dreary one and the girls were finishing off the leaflets and getting ready to send them out. The day was spent on the bus and Luci had put the television on, it ran on a battery and Jip always had a stock of live ones, he would charge them with his small solar panel. The television was due to stage a report on the meeting over section 48. It came on at six o'clock; the bus was packed with people who were all eager to watch!

"Fury erupted as the Government officials outlined criminal activities from within the protesters camp! Five have been arrested and the crown prosecution service has given its consent for them to be sent to trial! This could have a catastrophic effect on the final outcome of this protest! A census has officially been produced and a vote will go ahead tomorrow!"

The television went on to explain the plight of the Hill and section 48 and it interviewed opposing political parties. Twenty five minutes they answered questions and it was finalised with,

"Are the protesters becoming far from peaceful or are they're underlying feelings of frustration on their part, we shall have more on this tomorrow night at the same time."

Suzie switched the television off and Judy declared,

"They are trying to make us out as terrorists!"

The women spent the night paranoid and the three of them were so wound up that they all huddled into Luci's bed and they slept.

THE OTHER SIDE OF THE LINE

CHAPTER TWENTY ONE

"I can not believe you! Are we really to be stranded here!" Jip screamed as he realised the mess he was in.

The Colonel told him to shut up and a giant guard pushed him through another solid metal door, it had an electronic keypad, which the Colonel typed in a few numbers, and it opened.

Once they were inside, they found themselves in a sealed room and they felt the ship tilting slightly each way.

"I don't like this Jip!" Casy said as he fell against the metal walls.

It was not long and the Colonel reappeared with two different burly looking guards,

"These men are your mothers! Anything that you request will be given careful consideration and fulfilled if it is classed as reasonable, their decision is final, do you all understand?" The Colonel was as if he was speaking to some children!

Jip was not impressed nor were the others, they were all led then to a reception area, they all had to strip off and be examined by a toothless old doctor, he looked as if he came from the ark! Jip thought.

Jip complained and was told to shut up or be shut up, he chose the latter. When the medical was over, they were led into another hall way and through yet another steel door, when they entered they were face with a wide set of metal steps, it was all lit up like a hospital at night and it was dull and dingy.

"How old is this ship?" Casy asked trying to be polite.

"First world war! It went to Borneo!" The guard said acting smart.

The guard then pushed his chest out and ordered the men to walk into the hold.

"Spooky!" Jip said as they reached the bottom.

The guard then led them to another metal door and inside they saw a hold that was divided into two levels with little cells lining the edges. The two decks had ten cells and on the bottom deck.

There was a utilities room and a table tennis table!
The guard then opened yet another door, which revealed a spiral staircase, and he ordered them down them one at a time. Jip went down first, as he happened to be first there. When they had all reached the bottom they looked up and saw at least six guards all looking at them as if they were pigs gone to the slaughter! There was a loud clang and they found themselves all stood staring at each other in the hold.
"Jip is that you!" Came a voice Jip had not heard for a while.
"Dave! How? When?" Jip said as he saw Dave appear from the end cell.
Dave explained that he had been moved from the prison about a week ago and he had not seen a guard for a week! They all hugged each other and Dave revealed his knowledge of the place with them.
"We have to cook for ourselves, the food is delivered daily or it has been and all of our eating utensils are plastic!" Dave was excited to have his friends to talk with.
Neither Jip nor Casy had ever been in any prison before! They were taken in by it all.
"This is the best!" Dave said as he beckoned them all to the toilet area.
Inside were the normal urinals and five toilets. There was a shower room with a clothes washer that was useful Jip thought. Dave pointed out a hole that was in the side of the ship, it was about two inches round and he had been trying to open it more! Jip was first to look out and he saw the sea slapping just below the hole.
"Is that safe?" Jip asked Dave.
"When it is high tide as it is now the water is usually about two or three inches from the bottom of the hole, if we have strong waves then I have this metal board to cover it!"
Dave said as he produced a piece of steel board from behind the washer. Dave then offered them all a drink and he led them to the utility room.

THE OTHER SIDE OF THE LINE

He switched the boiler for the hot water on and he waited for it to tell it was ready before he made the drinks, hot and wet was Jip's thoughts as he drank his, Casy went and found a cell on the opposite side from where Dave had chose his. John went next to where Jip had decided he was going to sleep. They all then went to their cells and they slept.The next morning they were all woke with the load banging noise of the door opening at the top and a guard shouted,
"Come on! Go to the tray lift and collect you food and clothing packages!" The men all filed over to the tray lift and they waited as the packages were hauled down one at a time.
They took the boxes to the utility room where they unpacked them and placed all of the contents into the one cupboard that was there. Dave suggested a roister and he said that he would make the breakfasts. As they all started to eat their food, they heard the sound of the little boat moving away from the bigger ship.
"That's it, we are on our own for the day! Come with me!" Dave said and he beckoned them all to a red button that was on the spiral staircase.
Dave pressed the button and a computer type voice loudly said,
"You are under computer control, if there is an emergency press the button three times and you will be contacted to the supervisor. If you make a false call you will lose your food parcels for a day"
Jip laughed and he said he was going back to sleep and that was what he did do, they now had blankets and that meant a warm bed if not comfortable. Jip re-awoke at around two o'clock and his first reaction after a cup of tea was to get some fresh air.
He was starting to feel claustrophobic!
Casy and John had been messing around in the shower room trying to escape, but it was not happening! So they joined the two others.
It was not until four o'clock that the now familiar banging noise disturbed them.
"Come on you rabble! Time for you to get some exercise!" The voice boomed through the hollow decks.

They were then told to walk up the spiral steel staircase, one at a time. Jip went up first and it was a slow affair as his leg was hurting. When he finally manage to get to the top, Dave was moaning at him! Casy joined in with some laughter!

When they had all reached the top, they were shown into a room through another steel door. The four of them sat on a round bench and waited. Five minutes later a guard brought in a box of Wax waterproof jackets. They were all given one each, Casy and Dave did have to do a swap, as one was the bigger!

Once the excitement had calmed over the wax jackets. The men were again led by the guard, through two more steel doors and up another set of metal steps, they found that they could see through the next door! They all gasped the air as they entered the Cage.

The guards had hung a sign that stated the fact.

Jip stared about, it was like a playground when you were younger, he thought to himself quietly. All he saw was a wire fence that was all around the fifty or so foot pen! He went over to the side and he tried to clamber up the mesh, he wanted to see the ship they were on! Dave came to his rescue and he lifted Jip onto his shoulders so that he could take a look around!

Jip stared down the length of the ship; it was a mass of rust! Along side Jip saw a floating pontoon. The steel boat was just leaving the pontoon and it went right under to where Jip was hanging!

"I could have leapt on to that! If my leg did not hurt!"

Jip started moaning. Dave placed him back onto his feet and walked off. Casy was doing about the same as he scouted the space; he actually could pin point where the hole that Dave had made was! After two hours of not getting any where the men decided to come to the conclusion that they wont do it without any tools, not yet anyway. They all were staring towards the coastline; it was getting fainter as the evening's veil was pulling in. They then heard the dull thudding of a diesel engine. They all watched as the steel boat returned, as the boat manoeuvred on to the pontoon.

The water could be heard slapping, the sea was actually getting rougher as evening closed in. It must have taken the boat around ten minutes to actually get tied on to the pontoon! The four of them watched as the hatch opened and out stepped around twenty or so guards! A couple of them spat over the side in a gesture of some form! When a light was shone down onto the boat, Jip could see that the boat had eyes painted on the front and it was really strange to see! Jip shuddered; it was really cold where they were out in the sea air. It was about another ten or fifteen minutes later and the Cage was opened and they were escorted into the room with the round bench. Then they were escorted a bit roughly back into the hold! The men were able to take the jackets with them back into the hold and it was Jip's turn to cook the food tonight! Jip made a supper and they all ate heartily, they all decided on a quiet night and they went to their allotted cells. The night was becoming a rough one as the wind howled strongly and the ship rocked quite stubbornly in a rhythm. Jip could make out the sound of the rain as it was blown across the decks! Jip finally slept after staring into the metal clad walls for at least two hours.

It was four o'clock in the morning, the wind was at gale force and the ship creaked with every movement! The loud banging noise of the upper level door opening, woke the men. All the lights were then turned on. Jip met the other three as soon as he was dressed; they all stood watching as ten guards carrying truncheons descended down the stairway!

"Right you lot! Stand in a line against the wall!"

One of the guards screamed at the men.

The four followed the order and stood and faced the ten guards, each had a look of --

'Your scum!'

Written on their faces.

"So you lot think you can take us on? Let us see what you're made of you hippies!"

The guard shouted as the ten of them waded into the unarmed four. Jip dived at them as did Dave and they managed to grab a truncheon some how! The four took a step back and they faced the ten guards, the guards were looking angry, they waded in again, only this time they were much more serious. Jip was battered to the floor; the last thing he saw was a pair of boots that were heading for his face! Dave was actually holding his own, he was overpowered after Jip and Casy had been dragged into a cell to sleep off their hammering! Dave though would not give up! John tried to help him, but he was not a lot of use with his sore shoulder! For a second or two there was panic amongst the guards, but they soon got the better of Dave and John! John was the next to be invited for an early sleep! When he was dragged into the same cell as the other two. Jip opened his eyes, he leapt with all his might at the two guards who were carrying John, then after a brief struggle he was knocked back into Noddy land as he was smashed over the head with a truncheon from behind! Dave had again managed to get one of the truncheons! He was putting it to good use, that was until he was forced to the floor, after a flying kick from one of the guards, the rest of the guards started kicking the fallen Dave, but he still stood back up when they had finished. The guards decided that they would throw him into the same cell as the other three men. The door was slammed closed behind as Dave flew in, then the lock was heard to clank! It was the first time that the cell door had been locked.

"Shit I hurt!" Dave said as he saw Jip struggling to get up from the deck.

"I could do with a smoke!" Jip said as he sat on the only bunk bed.

There was then a rattle on the cell door; Jip sat with his back against the bulkhead.

"Here! You have earn't these!" A guard shouted and he threw in a packet of cigarettes.

Jip staggered to retrieve the packet and when he did, he found that there were only two broken cigarettes in the box.

"Cheers!" Jip spoke through his swelling fat lip!
The guards were then heard to walk back up the metal stairway and the loud banging of the door closing behind the last guard was heard. The four battered men, laid in silence in the locked cell, they all had their own pain to master. Jip fell asleep on the bunk and when Casy had come to, he saw that Jip had two blankets. He grabbed one trying not to disturb him. Jip did stir a little but Casy was successful in gaining a blanket!
"Another fine mess, hey Stanley?" Dave laughed at John who was looking rather sore!
The men all fell to sleep.
It was two hours later that the lights were switched on,
"Come on you rabble! The doctors here!" The familiar guard said.
None of the four men moved, the guard took this as a no go and he left the hold.
"Psycho!" Jip shouted as the loud bang was heard.
The four slept for about another two hours, it was nine o'clock when they were again woken. This time they were forced to go out into the cage, it was quite a task as the men were hurting and in sleep mode. The guards forced the men out on to the platform and they banged the door closed after them. It was pouring down with rain and the wind was still blustering! Dave was the most together and he led them all to a sheltered spot, well it almost was sheltered! The men sat and huddled together. They heard the boat start it's deep thudding engines and they watched as it managed to free itself into the open sea!
Jip mention that he would not want to meet that lot of guards again. They had noticed two guards as they crawled into the steel boat!
Dave stuck his two fingers up in a defiant manner, he was not seen, but the thought was there anyway!
It seemed to the four that they were left out in the freezing cold winds and rain for hours! It was the familiar guard who beckoned them to go back in.

"When you get back into the hold, pick up your supplies at the top level cells" The guard instructed them.

So the four wounded men had the added pressure of having to carry boxes of supplies down the steel stairway. Jip had become used to his pain and he was the first to take a box down. John managed one as did the other two.

Once they had retrieved the six boxes and placed them into the utility room, Jip opened the first one. Inside was packed with tobacco! This was a great surprise to them all and they shared out each packet amongst them. The other boxes contained, toilet paper, not very soft! There were all foods, drinks and two tin openers amongst the stash.

As the men unpacked everything, they were actually beginning to smile at each other, a strange humming sound was heard,

"The supplies you have been issued with are for the duration, we hope of your stay" A weird sounding voice said.

Jip mentioned to Dave that there were not really a lot of supplies, so he thought that it meant they were not staying too long on the prison ship! Dave dismissed the thought and said that he thought that they were the rations! They were so distracted that they never heard the steel boat returning. John decided that he would cook a big tea and he went about his duty. Jip and Casy sat and had a smoke and a cup of freeze-dried coffee each! Dave had found one of the metal tin openers and he had gone to the shower room and he tried to slice open his little hole. The tin opener snapped and he had to explain it to the others. He did that as they all ate the prepared tea,

"Don't worry we have another one!" John laughed as Dave showed his guilt.

While Jip and Casy were washing up after the meal, the loud banging was heard again. The noise had now become a warning sound and all four of the men waited and listened to the footsteps.

They were all surprised to hear single steps and Dave was the first to go out into the hold to see who it was.

"Dave is that you?" Said a familiar voice.

It was Jed!

Jed explained that Helen and he had gone to the meeting in London and were caught taking photographs and he stated that he was annoyed at losing his camera! He told that Helen had escaped and he asked why they were all battered and looking so rough! He mentioned that he had seen twenty or so guards get off of the steel boat, he also told them that he too had not been charged and had not been allowed a solicitor!

The evening was then spent discussing the Hill and the women! The days seemed to whittle away and every night for five nights.

One of them was taken out into the hold in the middle of the night and hosed down with a hosepipe! It was torture and hell and the men were starting to become very anti guards!

THE OTHER SIDE OF THE LINE

THE OTHER SIDE OF THE LINE

CHAPTER TWENTY TWO

Alex had been back to London, he had found out that Jip and the others had been taken to a prison ship! He did not know where the ship was docked when he had visited the Hill and told the women.
Judy and Luci had telephoned every organisation that they could and they had been informed that there was a prison ship docked at Southampton docks!
The last couple of weeks had taken there toll on Luci and she was near to snapping point, she had spent the time visiting Elaine and helping to organise the solstice party. Suzie had been a tower of strength, she was there helping Luci whenever she needed help. Luci had kept a diary and she was sat writing in to it. She wrote,

> Although time passes like the morning tide
> I still can't help the feeling inside
> All of the hurt and pain
> Will I ever hold you again?

It was only two days before the planned debate was to be had in parliament. Luci and everyone else were not happy, they had been told that they would not be able to attend, as only legal representatives would be allowed access. The highlight of the day came when Helen appeared! Judy had thought that she had been arrested in London. It was a nice feeling they all had to see her! She told them all of her struggle to escape and how the police had been rough to Jed!
Luci and Suzie spent the evening in the village and they went to the Valleydale arms where they saw some of the drinkers from the Hill. Luci had a discussion with one of the girls who she had seen but not often had time to sit and talk with her.
"If we do get evicted, it will be another Beanfield incident!" The girl said.

THE OTHER SIDE OF THE LINE

"That will never happen! We have legal representation that will fight for us!" Luci said feeling a touch of deja-vu as the girl spoke.

After the drink, Suzie and Luci retired to the bus and Luci telephoned Elaine who told her, Alex had been called away to London for the debate, she swore that he had promised to tell them the reactions as soon as they were had. She also told them that there was no public gallery and it was suggested that everyone stayed at the Hill!

The rest of the evening was spent with the two women discussing the party and the debate was put on hold! Later that evening and Luci had a strange telephone conversation! Todge had rang her and informed her that Jip and the others were in prison awaiting trial and they were all in good spirits she was told! He did not mention any visiting rights, but he did say that they would see each other very soon? Luci asked him on the last point. The telephone went dead before she had received an answer..

She screamed an insult down the empty telephone line and promptly slammed the unit onto her bed.

The next day was alive on the Hill, everyone was arriving and the people were setting up the Hill for the Solstice party! The café was having a new stage built and there was a lot of stalls being erected everywhere, some of the people who lived on the Hill had made custom jewellery from stones and clay using an earth kiln. Luci spent the morning at the site office and the afternoon she fed and walked Casy's Horses. The evening was spent with Judy and Suzie painting some new signs for the traffic they were to expect for the party, which was the next day! So was the start of the debate due in London.

CHAPTER TWENTY THREE

The day was Friday. Luci had woken; she saw a lot of vehicles all queuing up to get on to the Hill! It was just like a festival!
A bus had stopped next to Jip's and Luci had gone and met her old friend Stacey who was interested to hear all of the news about Jip and Casy. Stacey was a bit put off by the talk of police and Government, but she stayed to enjoy the party with her children.
When Luci went and visited Judy at the site office, she was given the job of organising some people to go on traffic duty.
Judy told her that she was a little worried about the amount of police that were at the bottom of the Hill, and in the village!
"They just hate to see people having a good time!" Luci told her.
Judy then explained to Luci that a few of the bands had not made it or they were late arriving, this gave Luci something else to do and she delegated a woman called Anne to do the traffic organising!
Luci found Suzie and the pair went around the site finding people who had musical instruments, they asked them all if they wanted to play and they sent them to the café.
It was not long and the music had begun and people were starting to congregate around the café. Luci and Suzie decided that they would check back with Judy, to see if any of the bands had arrived.
At the office they found Judy who was just finishing an important telephone conversation.
"That was the police! They have told me that they are not letting anymore vehicles up onto the Hill, any others would have to use the car park in the town and walk up!" Judy told the two women.
Luci was more interested in whether the bands had arrived. Judy finally said that they had and that they were parked behind a removal van, which had arrived. She stated that there was three different bands and asked if that would be enough? Luci told her, it was plenty and she went to find them. Suzie followed Luci and soon they were over speaking with the bands.

THE OTHER SIDE OF THE LINE

After a while all of the equipment was transferred to the stage at the café and the music began! Luci and Suzie decided to find out some of their old friends and they went on the hunt. The music was played all night and come early in the morning, a rave tent had been erected, Luci and Suzie had stayed up most of the night dancing, the pair were worried about the legality behind the rave! Yet seeing more people arrive and everyone enjoying him or herself, they forgot about the issue and they continued to dance to the heavy bass sounds. They danced for quite a few hours!

The party by then was in full swing, it had bands, the rave, and lots of people with smiling faces all having fun! Luci began to lose interest in the party as her heart was wishing Jip was with her, she knew he would have loved this successful gathering. She gradually became more upset and she returned to the bus and spent time reading Jip's old songs. She could see in her mind, Jip's face and she heard his voice singing as she read.

>When we are together we are so alive
>If we ever do part, I know I won't survive
>Oh, for the love of a dangerous mind
>And the strength of the older kind
>
>Tonight we are alone and we are free
>Away from society
>Out in the fields running free
>Away from society.

Tears filled Luci's eyes and she fell asleep listening to the thud of the bass sound. The party rocked on through the night as Luci slept.

There was at least one thousand people of all ages, sizes, and shapes all about. Fire jugglers were putting on shows; they were awesome as the flames silhouetted against the star lit sky. The best fact was that there was no violence! Just people enjoying the fun!

THE OTHER SIDE OF THE LINE

Suzie woke Luci at about six in the morning, Suzie was a little bit drunk and it was her turn to feel sad. Luci made her some coffee and the girls made a pact to go to Southampton and see the ship once the party was over! Luci felt a positive surge that ran across her body like a tornado. Suzie as she was feeling better, suggested that the two go for a walk. They left the bus and walked passed Stacey's bus, as they did they heard her shouting at some man and they ran in to find out what was going on. Stacy was in bed with three men! She was shouting in pleasure not pain! Luci and Suzie giggled and left her to it! When they had quickly left Stacey, they bumped into Judy who was busy checking everything.

The three of them strolled down the Hill, there was so much happening, slowly the girls began to feel at peace and they went to the café where a blues band had just started to play.

Luci and Judy started dancing while Suzie organised some warm drinks. They happened to be brandy coffees and soon the women were giggling to each other. After a while they decided to check Casy's Horses, one of Casy's friends had tethered the Horses to his cart and he politely offered the women a tour of the site. The three accepted and they leapt onto the flat bed trailer. Trundling along, the women witnessed people all sat around carefully prepared outdoor fires. Not far away were two clowns who were doing rolly polly's off of each's shoulders, they did it in a continuous way and the women laughed so much that Judy actually fell off of the trailer!

She had trouble catching it back up! Luci screamed with laughter, as did Suzie. Judy did not laugh as much but at least she saw the funny side!

When the trailer passed by the clowns, the women were sprayed with ribbons that the children had made, someone placed a crate of lager onto the trailer.

Luci stated that she felt a bit like a queen and they all gave the queens formal wave! The woman all broke open cans of the lager and they drank.

When they arrived at the café again a Celtic rock band was performing. After a couple more of the brandy coffee's the women were laughing and dancing, the music was great and it was only about eleven o'clock in the morning! The girls danced on into the afternoon and another group of women joined them. They all had a great time! After the band had finished, the party of women went back to Jip's bus with Luci and Suzie.
"Hey! Suffragettes can we join!" A group of men shouted as they all staggered passed them.
"It's a woman only campaign!" Judy shouted back at the men.
Once they had reached the bus and all of the women had entered, Luci thought of how Jip would have loved this, all of those women on his bus! The women talked and had fun without the complications of men. It was early evening by the time that they had all sobered up and someone suggested that they go and watch the famous rock band that were playing that evening!
The band was great and everyone enjoyed himself or her. Luci left early and she returned to the bus and crashed out in her bed listening to the rave music. Around mid-night and the rave was pumped up to a faster rhythmic beat, flashing lights filled the sky and everyone that was there had the best party they had ever had! Luci was oblivious to any extra noise and around ten o'clock the next morning, she was disturbed by the sounds of vehicles moving, she looked out of the window of the bus, she saw a convoy of buses and lorries all waving and tooting their horns as the left.
Luci dressed and went to the site office where she found Judy who was in a bit of a state.
"The police are in the village in force!"
Judy said solemnly as Luci entered.
Luci said she was more concerned with getting information from Alex and she asked if he had arrived yet? She was told that there was no sign of him. Luci then found Suzie who had slept in Casy's tree house alone!

"It is good old clean up day!" Luci said.

The two headed back to the bus and it was about an hour later that the last vehicle had left the site.

With the site back to normal, it was time to access any damage. They found none! So the women retired to the bus again and started working on the plan of getting to Southampton. They were well involved in the topic when Judy came clambering into the bus!

"Luci! The police are everywhere, they are getting bigger!"

Luci looked out of the buses front windscreen and she saw outside of the gate was around three hundred police officers all geared up for a riot it seemed!

"Maybe they are exercising!" Suzie said trying to calm the women.

"What with Helicopters!" Judy screamed as she watched.

Suddenly all hell broke lose as the helicopters flew over the Hill and they dropped in what looked like soldiers from ropes.

Men started to appear and they started to smash up people's benders and before the girls could do anything, the police had streamed forward and were rounding everybody up! A group of policemen started to tear Casy's tree house down while another group led the Horses away! Luci, Judy and Suzie watched in disbelief as the site office was tore apart and paper was strewn everywhere!

The girls were scared out of their wits as the windows of Jip's bus started to come crashing in!

"Quick! The emergency exit!" Luci screamed and led all of the women to the driver's door.

The women just got out as about fifteen police officers stormed onto the bus, they started to smash everything that was in their path!

Luci led the two women to the LandRover and she started the engine, "Drive! Luci drive!" Suzie screamed as she leapt in.

Luci did! She drove to the highest part of the Hill and they watched as the Hill village was dismantled and torn down. Women and children were being separated from their men folk and the men were being thrown into coaches, which had filled the lane!

Then the LandRover was suddenly surrounded and the police did not care that there were women on board as they smashed the windows and dragged the scared women out as if they were the scum's of the earth!
"Slow down you bastards!" Luci screamed as she was being dragged. The women were put with the other women on a separate coach to the men, they were told to sit near to the front and they were handcuffed together.
"You won't pass go! And you aren't getting any two hundred quid!" One of the policemen cockily stated.
Luci was in tears as she saw council wagons and refuse lorries arrived to clean up her home!
It did not take long and the coach they were on started driving down the Hill. It pulled up into the Valleydale car park and the women were allowed to use the toilet, with a woman police officer as guard!
Then as the three coaches left the car park, Luci stared back at the Hill. She was astounded to see that not one bender or tree house was stood. Even the giant marquee tent that was the café had been torn to the ground. She sat back into her seat and she wept. Nearly all of the other women did the same as the coach travelled out onto the motorway. The coach travelled for hours and the women became tired and slept. When they finally arrived amongst the company of police cars and pressmen. Luci woke to see the sight of the prison ship far out at sea!

THE OTHER SIDE OF THE LINE

CHAPTER TWENTY FOUR

Jip, Casy, John, Dave and Jed where all doing the same day in, day out routine of serving on the prison ship. The supplies had dwindled and the boredom was getting at them!
This morning had a very strange start to the day; the men had been awoken early and instructed to clean the hold, as they were to expect some new inmates!
The men discussed the possibilities of the new inmates as being murderers or even worse, Nonce's!
They all had their food and they went about cleaning, they scrubbed and washed everything that they could see.
After a few hours of that, they were taken up to the Cage out on deck, it was a clear day and not as cold as they had previously encountered. The men had by know become accustomed to the view of the shore and of the menacing looking steel boat. They watched the boat leave for the shore.
The hours whittled away and the men started to moan at each other, over the time they had to spend outside, it was becoming closer to their lunchtime. When they were instructed to go in for the lunch, the men all saw that the guard had been quadrupled!
Jip thought of the hammering that they had when the guards swelled before in numbers! Not one of the guards spoke to them; they were escorted back to the hold.
After the food, the now familiar guard came into their utility room,
"We are putting you out in the cage this afternoon, you will witness the arrival of the new inmates. I am sure you won't mind as I tell you that it will be from now on a mixed sex prison! The women will be allocated the top floor of the hold! Any indulgences will be classed as punishable offences, I mean that you would be sent to a high security prison on the main land." The guard said in a robot fashion.
The men all nodded their heads in confirmation of what had been said.

"It must be Christmas!" Dave said.

The men were then taken again to the Cage, this time they were given packets of cigarettes and they each had a carton of orange juice.

They all sat and stared through the wire mesh towards the shoreline. Dave was the first to notice the three coaches arrive on the dock.

On the shore, Luci, Suzie and Judy sat in the second coach. They were all preying that their loved ones were on the ship. Alex had told them that they were! Luci was still very upset and she felt a glimmer of hope that she might get to see Jip!

The same guard that had put them in the bus was there again. He instructed the women to stand out on the dockside. The women used the porta-cabin toilet one by one and sat looking at the steel boat as it docked. Ten of the men from the Hill, were the first to be placed onto the metal boat. The boat was lower in the water than Jip had ever seen it. When it arrived, Casy was first to spot that it was the men from the Hill!

"That's Marcus!" He shouted as he saw a man he knew well step out onto the pontoon.

Jip's heart murmured as he thought that the women were due, and could Luci be there?

Two more hours passed as they watched the steel boat make trip after trip to the shore and back to the ship. The sea was becoming a little more choppy when the last boat arrived on the pontoon, Jip knew that it must contain the women as he saw women guards emerging first. Luci was ushered out onto the platform with Suzie, the smell of the sea air, reminded Luci of her trip to Loch Ness with Jip. Then she was sure she heard him shouting to her!

She looked and saw a vague silhouette of him on the deck; he was frantically waving his arms. The woman guard told the women that they would have to share accommodation with the men! Luci was suddenly not afraid anymore! It took them around twenty minutes until they were placed into the hold. Luci saw Jip's cell as it had a pentagon scratched on the door.

She knew Jip always drew a pentagon on everything! She entered the cell and saw an unmade bed, she was then certain that the cell was Jip's. She sat on the bed and waited. Judy and Suzie did the same.

Jip and Casy were trying to knock the door down to get inside! It was ages until they were finally taken in; they were taken to see the governor! The men were offered paid jobs, six pound a week! To keep everyone in order and to handle the everyday running of the hold. The men all agreed and they signed a letter that was already formatted for them. They were told that they would have to run the tuck shop and that the supplies were due in the next day!

Then they were taken back to the hold, they all ran down the metal staircase and looking around the men did not see the women!

Jip took a deep breath and he walked into his cell, Luci was asleep on his bed and he did not disturb her, he just sat staring at her face.

"I have missed you so much" Luci said to him as they kissed and cuddled when she had opened her eyes.

Similar happenings were there for Casy, John and Jed.

Over food, the Hill, was the topic and Luci upset Jip when she told him,

"We have lost our fight, the Hill is no longer being held!"

Luci explained all of the happenings and Jip was so annoyed and he felt so frustrated as he was helpless!

That evening they all had each others company and most had an early night! The next day was a busy day for the original five men as they had to unload the boat with supplies for the shop and cutlery and blankets were unloaded on the second return of the boat. Dave was commissioned to run the shop and each of the prisoners was given credit of three pounds a week to spend.

Jip arranged a meeting, he said that he was proud of everyone and that they must all continue with the mood of survival! He thanked everyone for the support they had given the Hill! The days passed with each day being as boring as the first, Jip organised a three-legged race in the Cage one day and it became the highlight of that week.

He continued to run the race on every Tuesday and most looked forward to it!

Another week passed, only this week Jip and Casy were summoned to the governor's office, they were told that the properties that had been rescued from the Hill would be given to them. Jip was really pleased when the musical instruments were given to him! That evening Jip and John played music, everyone sat on the floor of the hold as Jip started to sing,

> It is such a sad affair, you shed your heart, they strip it bare
> Are you a stranger to this feeling or will it prolong being
> Will you be the same if I took your love and not believed you?

> You must be the spirit of an angel
> You must be a spirit of an angel, you are
> You must be a spirit of an angel, you are

> Why does the past never forfeit the path?
> Ever changing sights mark the belief in one delight
> We should have never of lost the fight
> Yet we will never give up our sight

> You must be a spirit of an angel, you are
> You must be a spirit of an angel, you are.

Jip and John then broke into a very long instrumental and the people started to dance and the spirit of the Hill was revived!

The people became more in touch as the weeks passed, Jip was still their leader and they respected him a great deal.

CHAPTER TWENTY FIVE

The Hill was desolate as Elaine walked her dog on it, the only people she saw was builders, who were erecting a wire fence in a straight line to the top of the ridge. Elaine sat by the big Oak that only two weeks ago was someone's home! On the floor she found a piece of rope which had a block of wooden peg tied onto it. She placed it into her pocket, and then she stumbled back to the library.

The builders were working around the clock; they were just about ready for the gas to travel along the pipes that they had laid!

It was a Tuesday when the grand turning on of the gas was arranged! The Hill was teaming with people again! Only this time they all were politicians and pressmen. Alex had been forced to attend; he was the councillor for Valleydale. It was a snooty affair, with the major; even the minister from London was there!

The top minister was to press a button that would officially open section 48!

"I am proud to be given the honour of declaring section 48 open!" The minister said as he pressed the button.

A weird humming noise came from the pump at the base of the Hill, A red liquid started to slowly travel up the laid down pipe and everyone watched as plummets of red gas was released at the top of the Hill!

The town was then host to a lavish feast and party at the Town Hall. Alex did not attend and he was meant to speak in favour of section 48. Alex was a touch taken back the next day when he received orders for him to attend a disciplinary hearing in London. He had to spend the rest of the week working out his reasons for the committee. He decided that he would visit the Hill and experience the effect that section 48 was making. Once he arrived at the new pump house, the first thing he noticed was the baroness of a few of the trees! The ones that were near to the top! He also found that his breathing became heavier the higher he climbed!

THE OTHER SIDE OF THE LINE

He wrote all of this down and it formed the basics of his defence for London.

Alex travelled up to the meeting in London and after he felt as if he did not agree with one thing that had been discussed! He thought of himself as a spoilsport.

It really was only one month from the turning on of the pump that it's sad effect was starting to take shape.

At first, it was Elaine who mentioned the rain! It had started to rain in intervals of three-hour stretches, having an hour dry to every three wet! That week some school children had also ran into the library crying, they were upset, on the way they passed the brook, they had saw fish, dead and floating on the surface. A few days later and Elaine had quite a shock!

Elaine had opened the library as normal and the morning had been raining on and off, she decided that she would go and check on Jip's bus for him, she always had a soft spot for Jip. She saw that nothing had been touched at Jip's bus, and when she returned to the library she was getting out of her car and the floor gave away beneath her stiletto heel!

She went immediately into the library and she telephoned the local garage.

"It's the bloody rain! I have so many welding jobs since they switched that bloody pump on! I can fit you in next Tuesday if you like Elaine?" The local mechanic said.

Elaine could not help thinking of the rain! She decided that she would grab a jam jar and get a sample of the rain! She thought that she would place it on the river bank away from peoples view, she did this and when she had found the spot where she was going to place the pot, she knelt down, she looked along the river bank, she was disgusted at what she saw! Horrified would be another way of expressing Elaine's feelings!

Lain on their backs with their legs in the air, were the four ducks that she always used to feed!

THE OTHER SIDE OF THE LINE

She ran straight into the library and tried to contact Alex! She had no joy, he was not at his office.
Elaine was quite distraught and after about two hours, she wrote a letter addressed to the minister in charge of section 48!
Alex visited Elaine later that evening and when she explained about her day, he stood up and stated,
"Enough is enough! Next it will be the children! I am going to create my own protest committee! Will you join me?"
Elaine showed him her letter and Alex left with a bee under his bonnet!The next monthAlex had formed the committee; it had sent shock waves through the conservative governing body.
Alex and his members were told to close down or resign! They did neither!
Alex did actually resign and he formed an organisation party to challenge the local council in the environmental avenues.
Alex had a great surprise when the opposition to the government leaders, contacted him and thought that his stand against the government would help them win the election, the election was a few months away at this time! The opposition party backed on the support they would create by abolishing section 48. Alex was to be their key!
Alex if he was honest thought of this as desperate measures to win votes, he decided to join them though. Alex started to gain evidence from the gas and the Hill. He was bemused at the depth of all of the facts. The by-election was to be run Wednesday next, Alex was running and he had a great chance of winning! He geared Elaine up to support him. She placed a few of Jip and Luci's leaflets into the library window again!
Alex was pleasantly surprised when the final of the by election was cast, he actually did win and he was given a plush new office.
He kept gaining support from every angle and he for the first time thought that they had a great chance of winning the main election.
The run up went quite crazy as the campaign twisted towards freeing the protesters against section 48.

Alex had his first contact with the prison ship to see how the place was being run; he was appalled at the rusting wreck!
This added more fuel to his campaign and he borrowed some of Jip's printing equipment and produced leaflets that read,

TAKE YOUR TIME TO THINK ABOUT THE ABOLISHMENT OF SECTION 48. FREE THE INNOCENCE OF THIS GOVERNMENTS MISTAKE!

THE OTHER SIDE OF THE LINE

The campaign was run for the last three weeks of the election, and it gathered support like a run away train. It was such a real happening as the children did start to vomit and the press had a field day.

Public opinion was so against it when light of the ill children hit the headlines! The government was forced to postpone any more of the pumping!

Alex then led a campaign to free the protesters from the prison ship and Elaine made a statement to the press which in its entirety, said that if the government was changed then the protester would be released if the party lost, then so would the protesters.

Jip and Luci and the others were only told of their peril the night before the general election!

THE OTHER SIDE OF THE LINE

CHAPTER TWENTY SIX

On board the vessel there was pandemonium! The guards were confused, were the prisoners to be released or not? A few were concerned about their jobs!
Jip, John, Casy, Dave and Jed were summoned in the evening of Election Day to see the chief governor!
The governor told the men that they would all be released in the morning! The men were instructed to have everyone packed and the place cleaned by ten o'clock the next morning!
There was great jubilation as Jip told the others of the change in government! And of how the changes affected them directly!
The evening was spent, all-preparing for the morning and later that night, Jip sang a song,

> We are to be set free
> We are to see our family
> We are to make them open their eyes
> It is our destiny
>
> They have lost and we have won
> The spell of nature has proved number one
> We fought for what we felt right
> Now we can dance in the sheltered light
> We are to be set free!

Jip played on for about two more hours, he sang a lot of anti government protest songs and even the guards came and listened!
No one could honestly say that they slept a lot that night, they were all so excited about being released in the morning!
When ten o'clock finally came, they were all taken one by one to the governors office, each was given a weeks dole money and a official pardon and sent out to the waiting boat.

There was no sign of the steel boat; in its place was a giant Motor Cruiser! Once Jip and Luci had joined it they were slap in the middle of a sea going party!

They all drank alcohol, the first time for many months, Casy raised his glass with the men and he looked at Jip and said,

"Cheers to our next crusade!"

They all drank a toast and ate some of the lavish food that had been laid on.

When the cruiser landed them on the shore, the dock was crammed with people's families and press and television cameras.

Jip stood with Luci and drinking a can of lager each, they shouted,

"Cheers to freedom!"

Later that day Jip and Luci finally arrived back at Valleydale and walking up to the bus Jip stated.

"Well, to work we must go"

THE END

ANCIANTICAL= MEANS LIVING THE ANCIENT WAYS....

To read Jip and Luci on their journey to Egypt and the imminent threats they encounter! Contact your local bookshop and order a copy now!

THE OTHER SIDE OF THE LINE-
The new BACKWARDS BUT LEFT=SCIENCE FICTION
AVAILABLE AUGUST 1999....

THE OTHER SIDE OF THE LINE